Stories by Contemporary Writers from Shanghai

BEAUTIFUL DAYS

T0206556

Text: Teng Xiaolan
Translation: Qiu Maoru
Cover Image: Getty Images
Interior Design: Xue Wenqing
Cover Design: Wang Wei

Assistant Editor: Wu Yuezhou
Editor: Susan Luu Xiang
Editorial Director: Zhang Yicong

Senior Consultants: Sun Yong, Wu Ying, Yang Xinci
Managing Director and Publisher: Wang Youbu

ISBN: 978-1-60220-235-1

Address any comments about *Beautiful Days* to:
Better Link Press
99 Park Ave
New York, NY 10016
USA

or

Shanghai Press and Publishing Development Company
F 7 Donghu Road, Shanghai, China (200031)
Email: comments_betterlinkpress@hotmail.com

Printed in China by Shanghai Donnelley Printing Co., Ltd.
1 3 5 7 9 10 8 6 4 2

Two Novellas

BEAUTIFUL DAYS

By Teng Xiaolan

Better Link Press

Foreword

English readers will be presented with a set of pocket books. These books contain outstanding novellas written by writers from Shanghai over the past 30 years. Most of the writers were born in Shanghai after the late 1940's. They started their literary careers during or after the 1980's. For various reasons, most of them lived and worked in the lowest social strata in other cities or in rural areas for much of their adult lives. As a result they saw much of the world and learned lessons from real life before finally returning to Shanghai. They embarked on their literary careers for various reasons, but most of them were simply passionate about writing. The writers are involved in a variety of occupations, including university professors, literary editors, leaders of literary institutions and professional writers. The diversity of topics covered in these novellas will lead readers to discover the different experiences and motivations of the authors. Readers will encounter a fascinating range of esthetic convictions as they analyze the authors' distinctive artistic skills and writing styles. Generally speaking, a realistic writing style dominates most of their literary works. The literary works they have elaborately created are a true reflection of drastic social changes, as well as differing perspectives towards urban life in Shanghai. Some works created by avant-garde writers have been selected in order to present a variety of styles. No matter what writing styles they adopt though, these writers have enjoyed a definite place, and exerted a positive influence, in Chinese literary circles over the past 3 decades.

Known as the "Paris of the Orient" around the world, Shanghai was already an international metropolis in the 1920's and 1930's. During that period, Shanghai was China's economic, cultural and literary center. A high number of famous Chinese writers lived, created and published their literary works in Shanghai, including, Lu Xun, Guo

Moruo, Mao Dun and Ba Jin. Today, Shanghai has become a globalized metropolis. Writers who have pursued a literary career in the past 30 years are now faced with new challenges and opportunities. I am confident that some of them will produce other fine and influential literary works in the future. I want to make it clear that this set of pocketbooks does not include all representative Shanghai writers. When the time is ripe, we will introduce more representative writers to readers in the English-speaking world.

Wang Jiren
Series Editor

Contents

Beautiful Days

1

While having supper, Old Lady Wei spied Yao Hong's hand on Wei Xingguo's thigh.

The table was square-shaped and the only thing that shielded her son's thigh was the one corner where the tablecloth hung down. But the tablecloth was not a screen as it was made of gauze and was clearly transparent, which was how Old Lady Wei was able to see what was going on.

Xingguo pretended as if nothing was happening. He kept on eating even though he was uncomfortable. Hong was a talented girl, to say the least. One moment she was serving soup to Old Lady Wei: "Mom, have more soup," and the next she was sliding her hand onto Xingguo's thigh. She accomplished all this without a hitch.

Old Lady Wei's eyes were ruler sharp and they surmised that Hong's hand was two centimeters above her son's knee. It was not on the most sensitive spot and it was still outside that forbidden part of his body. Old Lady Wei reckoned that it has only been less than a month since Hong came to live with them in their home. And it was only a short time ago that Xingguo had stuttered like a school boy upon meeting Hong.

At first, Hong behaved decently. When Old Lady Wei asked her to shake hands with her son, she simply refused, looking as shy and timid as a naïve virgin. What a different girl she was now!

When Old Lady Wei gave a slight cough, Hong withdrew her hand and begin serving soup to her again. "Here, Mom, have another bowl of soup."

Old Lady Wei gave a snort. She did not intend to call Hong out, but she wanted to give her a veiled warning. Didn't she know that when eating with elders, young people should restrain themselves?

Old Lady Wei cast her eyes at Hong. Not long after she came to Shanghai, Hong had learned to wear makeup. However, she did not paint her eyebrows evenly. As a result, the impression on her face came across confused. Old Lady Wei could not contain her amusement, but she also disdained Hong's behavior. In her mind, country bumpkins will always be country bumpkins. Plain country girls without any makeup are more tolerable than those who do not know how to apply it correctly.

Hong came recommended by their neighbor Auntie Zhang. Old Lady Wei did not like northerners and preferred a girl from Jiangsu or Zhejiang provinces. It was difficult to limit the candidate to these two provinces. The pretty girls from there would not choose Xingguo as their lifelong partner and ugly girls were not an option for Old Lady Wei. Auntie Zhang persuaded her to broaden her scope of selection. Those from farther away would appreciate even more Xingguo's status as a registered permanent resident of Shanghai. This particular circumstance would give him more candidates. It was just like multiplication equation: $X * Y = Z$. If Z is a constant, the smaller X is, the bigger Y will be. Old Lady Wei had to admit that Auntie Zhang's reasoning was right.

Auntie Zhang acted promptly and a few days later brought a photo to Old Lady Wei. The girl lived in Shangrao in Jiangxi Province. Old Lady Wei thought the she was passable in terms of appearance. She asked Auntie Zhang about her age. Auntie Zhang said she was 34 years old. Old Lady Wei asked if she had been married before. Auntie Zhang said she had been married. Old Lady Wei asked whether she had any children and Auntie Zhang told her no. Old Lady Wei wanted to know whether they were divorced or her husband was dead. Auntie Zhang said he had gotten ill and died two years ago.

Old Lady Wei paid for the girl's train ticket. She and Auntie Zhang agreed that the girl should come to Shanghai. Old Lady Wei told Auntie Zhang not to give the girl the impression that she would accept her as her daughter-in-law, because she was not sure whether she would like her or not. Auntie Zhang assured Old Lady Wei that she was aware of her all her concerns.

The girl lived several hundred kilometers away and it took the train the whole day to cover the distance. What's more, the girl was a complete stranger to them. If she were satisfactory, everything would go well. If she were not an ideal candidate, there would not be any leeway for Old Lady Wei would not compromise.

Auntie Zhang racked her brain and came up with a clever idea. She advised Old Lady Wei to start the girl off as a maid and pay her wages. If they liked her, Xingguo could marry her. If the girl was not to their liking, they could dismiss their maid anytime. This way, neither of them would suffer any losses.

Old Lady Wei appreciated Auntie Zhang's cleverness, but was concerned that it might wound the girl's pride and she would turn down their invitation. Auntie Zhang said every job candidate must pass the probation period. If the girl turned down their request, many more would be willing to take her place. She added that Xingguo could easily marry a Shanghai girl if he was not disabled. This would be a once in a lifetime chance for a girl from Shangrao, and she should rejoice over her good fortune.

The day after Hong's arrival Old Lady Wei brought her to the hospital for a physical check up. Though it may seem a little bit rude, she would not take a casual attitude toward her health. The fact that Hong did not have children saved all of them a lot of trouble. However, Old Lady Wei was worried that she might be sterile. Old Lady Wei was in her late sixties and was eager to have a grandchild. Her son was well over forty and could not wait any longer. If the girl was sterile, Old Lady Wei would not hesitate to dismiss her even if she looked as beautiful as a goddess.

The physical proved that she was a healthy girl.

Old Lady Wei explained to the girl that periodic physical examinations were routine in Shanghai.

When they got back home, Old Lady Wei vacated the small room facing north and turned it into Hong's bedroom. The tiny room was made from a hung cloth partition. The one-meter-wide single bed nearly occupied the whole space. Its former occupier was Xingguo, who moved to the attic. Hong sized up the renovated old house. Though small, the house had a gas range and private bathroom.

Old Lady Wei watched Hong unpack. Her old nylon bag contained a few pieces of clothing that were as old as one could imagine. Her Dacron bras were old fashioned and worn out from repeated washing. Even women of Old Lady Wei's age would not wear these kinds of bras. Hong did not even bring towels or toiletries. Old Lady Wei selected two new towels for her and told Xingguo to buy a toothbrush from the convenience store downstairs. She searched in the drawer and took out a new pair of silk pajamas that she had bought long, long ago. She presented this to Hong as a gift on that first meeting.

Hong was grateful for the gift. "Auntie, you're so kind to me."

Old Lady Wei told her to call her Mom, after all, Hong was not really a maid. She came all the way to Shanghai for the purpose of finding a husband. She should not be treated shabbily. It was customary in Shanghai for young people to address a woman of the older generation as Mom anyway. In the old days, Xingguo's classmates always addressed her as such. It didn't really mean what it does. Old Lady Wei wanted to show her good intentions by not treating Hong like a stranger in front of the neighbors.

Since Hong was not a maid at all, it was only natural for Old Lady Wei to mentally prepare for her less-than-satisfactory housework. As a native of Jiangxi Province, Hong liked rich and spicy food. Old Lady Wei warned her against putting fiery spices in the food. She also told her to add less oil and salt to the food. Hong readily obliged Old Lady Wei's request and the first meal cooked by her was as tasteless as boiled vegetables.

"Mom," she said as she set the dishes on the table. "I realize why Shanghai girls have such clear and milky complexions. It's because they eat bland food."

Old Lady Wei told her that mild taste didn't mean "tasteless." Her tasteless food was only for patients with a kidney disease.

The second meal prepared by Hong was typical Jiangxi cuisine. The spicy food brought tears and mucus to their eyes and noses. Old Lady Wei did not blame her, as she understood that Hong was too nervous to learn the proper way of cooking. Old Lady Wei started to teach her how to cook Shanghainese food from scratch. She showed her how to buy, select, cut, assort, and cook the food. The stir-fry celery and shredded pork dish was a tough one to prepare because of the celery. Every stalk had to be split and washed. It takes three or five washings to get half a bunch of celery ready for cooking. The pork should be cut into the width of the celery pieces. This way, the dish will look inviting. When the celery is sautéed, water will come out. After getting rid of the water, the celery is reduced to half a plate full.

The deep-fried lesser croakers, though cheap, was another time consuming dish. Every fish must first have its chest cut open and the belly slit to remove its internal organs. After washing them thoroughly under the tap, they have to be salted and hung up to dry for half a day. Then they're deep-fried one by one in boiling oil, their aroma permeating the whole kitchen. Patience must be employed during the deep-frying process, because if the fish is not heated in a balanced way, it won't be crispy on the outside and tender inside. The temperature of the cooking oil should not be too high, or the skin of the fish will burn.

Old Lady Wei chose these two dishes as an orientation course for a beginner like Hong. She wanted to pass on to her the essence of the Shanghainese way of living—elegant simplicity and exquisite pursuit.

Not wanting to burden Hong with anymore pressure, Old Lady Wei told her to do the housework the way she did it at home, because she did not want to burden Hong with more pressure. Hong kept that in mind but she did just the opposite. The mopping was a good example. Hong was hard working. She knelt down and mopped the floor with a wet rag. The rag was so wet that the floor looked like a piece of paper scattered with Chinese character strokes. Old Lady Wei told her to use the mop. With a mop, she could clean the floor thoroughly and easily. She need only clean the windows with newspapers once every month. The refrigerator should be defrosted every two months. The balcony should be swept daily. As for the laundry, she should separate underwear from other clothes. She should wash dark color and light color clothes separately in the washing machine, otherwise the latter will be tainted by the former. Sheets and quilt covers should be washed every two weeks. After they are dried in the sun, she should iron them to make them flat and smooth. She did not need to iron Old Lady Wei's clothes since the old lady didn't have any special visitors. However, she must see to it that Xingguo's shirts and jackets are well pressed. Though he worked in the janitor's room at a factory, all the staff and workers would see him when they entered.

Hong jotted down everything Old Lady Wei said. The latter was satisfied with her humble attitude despite not knowing her true motive. The right attitude was the prerequisite for positive action. When Old Lady Wei put the wage for the first month in front of Hong, she looked a bit shocked. She accepted the money after hesitating for few seconds. Her face became flushed.

Old Lady Wei felt a little guilty when she saw Hong's expression. It seemed that she had underestimated her. If it had been a Shanghainese girl, she would have turned and walked away. At the thought of this, Old Lady Wei spoke in a soft tone. "Please put down your mental burden and make yourself at home."

Hong called Xingguo "brother." When he met her for the first time, something bright, like a ray of light, flashed in his eyes and swiftly disappeared. Hong was normal when she talked with Old Lady Wei, but when she talked to Xingguo, she spoke with a twang as though she had a severe cold. Her nasal sound came out after vibrating repeatedly in her nose. It gave one an impression she was not speaking frankly. Infected by her twang, Xingguo spoke in a halting way and uttered a word or two after a long hesitation. Old Lady Wei was not pleased with their way of talking. But she realized that her son's preference was of prime importance. If he did not like her, Old Lady Wei could do nothing, because the days of arranged marriages were gone forever.

A draught ventilates Shanghai's lanes and no secret can be kept in such an environment. After a few days, every neighbor in the lane asked Old Lady Wei in a considerate tone: "She's come, hasn't she?"

Old Lady Wei nodded her head. "We'll wait and see."

Before her neighbors could bombard her with more questions, Old Lady Wei walked by swiftly. She did not want to talk about this subject because there was not the slightest sign of success yet. Those gossipy neighbors were good at turning rumors into truth. That was what Old Lady Wei feared most.

On the contrary, Hong was friendlier than one expected. She always politely exchanged greetings with the neighbors. Though she did not talk much, she was not oblivious either. She often lent a hand to their neighbors, such as helping them with shopping or hanging their laundry. As time passed, Old Lady Wei came to see her merits. Instead of the affected manner of most country bumpkins, she got along with people naturally. The embarrassing relationship that she was worried about did not materialize. Though she addressed her as "Mom," practical minded Hong never regarded herself as her daughter-in-law. She considered herself as an apprentice still in the probation period. A girl had to learn to be a qualified daughter-in-law. In Hong's mind, compared with her master in Shangrao, Old Lady Wei was kind enough to offer her board, lodging, and money. This put Hong's mind at eased.

Before she left Shangrao, Hong made detailed and thorough inquiries about the Wei family. She knew that the matchmaker was a hasty person. She could do nothing about that, but marriage was a matter of prime importance to her. She asked if Xingguo was born a cripple. The matchmaker said he was healthy when he was born. He became a cripple after he suffered from polio.

"How much does he earn a month?" Hong asked.

"One thousand yuan," the matchmaker answered. "That's the minimum wage in Shanghai."

Hong asked whether the Wei family owned their house and how big the house was.

"It's like those houses you see on TV in the old-style lanes," the matchmaker said. "The ones with an attic and a garret shared by different people. Can you imagine how big it is now?"

The matchmaker was a distant relative of Auntie Zhang. A dozen other girls were waiting for her to find them husbands and she could pick and choose which girl she would bestow help upon. It was obvious she was not enthusiastic about doing this favor of arranging Hong's marriage.

"If he is a healthy and handsome young man

earning more than twenty thousand yuan a month and living in a villa, do you think he is foolish enough to marry you?" The matchmaker said.

Hong was not offended by the matchmaker's words. Instead, she slipped a red packet to her under the table. "Please do your best for me."

Old Lady Wei and her son went to the railway station to meet Hong. Xingguo held a colorful placard high above the crowd: Yao Hong from Shangrao, Jiangxi.

Hong's first impression of Old Lady Wei was that she was neat and tidy, which gave her some relief because that meant she did not have to take care of her daily. She turned to Xingguo. When he stood, you couldn't tell he was a cripple. With a big nose and narrow eyes, he was not handsome, but he was by no means ugly. This gave Hong further relief.

They took a taxi even though the railway station was not far from their home. Xingguo sat in the passenger's seat and she and Old Lady Wei sat in the back seat. It was the first time that Hong had taken a taxi. She was so nervous that she sat against the door for fear of touching Old Lady Wei, who sat up straight and kept silent. Hong learned from the go-between that Old Lady Wei was retired accountant, which made her an educated woman.

Hong had nothing to do but look ahead. Xingguo was going bald on the back of his head. A small patch there exuded a brilliant shine. "Oh, and he has favus on his head also," Hong thought to herself.

She was pleased with the fact that both the mother and son went to the railway station to meet her.

"I was so touched you came all the way to meet me," she gushed profusely to Old Lady Wei about this incident later. "You are old and Brother is clumsy in the leg, yet you came all the way to meet me. I was really touched when I saw you both."

Old Lady Wei shook her head modestly. "You came to Shanghai from so far away and it was only right for us to meet you at the railway station. It's just being courteous."

"That's why I was so deeply touched."

She used the word "touched" another three times and by the end, she was on the verge of tears. It was only good manners to exaggerate other people's kindness. There was nothing to lose in pleasing others. In her letter to her parents, she told them she called Xingguo "Brother," which make her relatives in

Shangrao laugh. "How come you call him Brother? He is your husband, not your brother."

"Yes, he is my husband," she explained. "I mean for it to imply that he was my sweetheart brother. I think it's appropriate and gives a certain intimacy, but it doesn't sound embarrassing. It's simple and uncomplicated. I like it."

The second week after Hong came to their home, Xingguo invited her out to watch a matinee, which was only half price since it was in the morning. They were the only two people in the movie theatre. As soon as the lights dimmed and the movie began, Xingguo started to touch Hong. At the first, he skimmed her lightly as if by accident so he could see her reaction. Hong responded by moving to the other side of her seat. But the space was cramped, so she gave up dodging Xingguo's hands, which got bolder and bolder as they moved all over her as his eyes pretend to focus on the screen. Hong tried with all her self-control to suppress a laugh. She did not want to embarrass the both of them, especially not then and there.

The problem was the space in their house. It was tiny. It would have been fine if it was just the two of them, but Old Lady Wei's presence restricted their freedom. There was a rumor that the government planned to dismantle the old houses on their block. But as the saying goes, there is much talk but little done, and the plan was shelved. So Xingguo decided to take matters into his own hands. He had learned from some of the young workers in the factory the ways they went about dating their girlfriends. One method in particular only required a dozen yuan, which would put you and your date in a movie theatre for two hours. It was much cheaper than going to a café. As it was, the nearby theatre was running a promotion and charged only ten yuan for the ten o'clock morning show.

Xingguo had to ask Old Lady Wei for money to go to the movies. He gave his wages and disability subsidies to his mother. He did not smoke or drink. He only spent money haircuts and DVDs. Old Lady Wei gave him a hundred yuan and Xingguo asked her for more. She gave him another hundred, but he was not satisfied.

Old Lady Wei looked at him curiously. "Why do you need so much money?"

Xingguo blushed. "I'm going to the movies."

Old Lady Wei made sure to ask the question in front of Hong. She knew that they were going to the movies, but she did not approve of it. However, when she heard her son telling the truth, she felt sorry for him. It was embarrassing for a 40-year-old man to ask his mother for pocket money. Old Lady Wei gave him another hundred yuan.

"Why don't you go to the park?" Old Lady Wei suggested. "Sitting in the park, even for the whole day, won't cost you a penny."

Xingguo only mumbled unintelligibly.

"Mom is right," Hong chirped in. "I had been thinking the same thing."

"You really know how to play innocent," Old Lady Wei thought, but did not say out loud, as she cast a sidelong glance at Hong.

That first time was followed by a second time and then a third. Xingguo's demand increased each time and became quite frequent, putting Old Lady Wei in a sullen mood. Finally, Xingguo told her that he wanted to take care of his own wages. His wage was thirteen hundred yuan and the monthly disability subsidy was over two hundred yuan. That put his monthly income over fifteen hundred yuan. "I'm not a kid. I feel stupid asking you for pocket money."

Old Lady Wei flatly refused. "You're still a kid until you get married. I'll keep the money for you. Just ask me for it when you need it. Don't you trust me?"

"It has nothing to do with trust," Xingguo tried to explain. "I don't think it's necessary. You're getting old and it's a hassle to take care of my money."

Old Lady Wei sighed. "I don't think it's a hassle. Using my brain will keep me from becoming senile. Counting banknotes will keep my hands from getting frostbite."

Xingguo was at a disadvantage. He turned his eyes to the kitchen. Hong was cooking behind the closed door. It was only Old Lady Wei and her son in the living room. Old Lady Wei knew Hong wanted to avoid arousing suspicion. The more she tried to cover it up, the more conspicuous she became.

A moment later Hong brought out the cooked food and set it on the table. Her cooking skills had improved. The crucian carp with green onions looked very enticing. The only problem was her liberal use of MSG, which made them thirsty afterwards. When she suffered from severe lower back pain a couple of years ago, Old Lady Wei hired a maid to take care of her.

The maid also liked to put MSG in every dish. This was the common fault of maids. Since they were not chefs, they have to put MSG in the food to conceal their poor cooking skills. Old Lady Wei had warned Hong several times. Though she promised she would follow her advice, she would sprinkle MSG on the cooked food anyway. This had become her usual practice.

"You'll get kidney stones if you eat too much MSG," Old Lady Wei told her.

"Mom, spare me your over exaggerations," Xingguo said. "MSG is not poison."

Old Lady Wei gave her son the evil eye. "Everything has a limit. If you exceed it, even the fountain of youth will kill you."

Hong kept silent, knowing very well that Old Lady Wei was making these comments for her benefit. Xingguo asked his mother for money more and more frequently, even proposing to take care of his own money. It was only too natural for the old lady to think that he had exceeded the limit.

After cleaning up the dining table, Hong went to collect the laundry from the balcony. Old Lady Wei was taking a sweater apart and asked for her help.

"Are you going to knit something?" Hong asked.

"I'm going to knit a scarf for Xingguo."

"My sight is better than yours, Mom. Let me knit it for him."

Old Lady Wei relented and handed the ball of wool to her. She sat back as Hong started to knit. They watched a Korean drama called *Men at the Bathhouse Owner's Family* on TV.

"Korean people have good manners. The younger members of a family always obey their elders," Old Lady Wei said, breaking the silence. "Not like in China, the roles have been reversed."

"China has the same roles."

Old Lady Wei heaved a long sigh. "There's a popular saying in Shanghai: 'If you want to find peace in a family, the elder members should act like juniors.' That's the case with me. I have to act like a junior, because juniors ride roughshod over seniors."

Xingguo was reading a newspaper off to the side, pretending as if he hadn't heard anything. Old Lady Wei was so agitated that she nearly choked and started coughing. Hong put down her knitting and went to the kitchen to pour a cup of tea. "Mom, have some tea."

Old Lady Wei took the cup. When she saw Hong's fearsome look, she said to herself: "Don't act like a bullied child bride." Then Old Lady Wei cast her eyes at her son. Compared the little woman, he looked simply like a stupid scatterbrain. At the thought of this, Old Lady Wei was even more unwilling to let her son take care of his money. Her son's money was much the same as the little woman's money. If anything went wrong, the consequences would be costly.

Xingguo put down the newspaper and went up to his attic with a plastic bag of thin bamboo strips. Old Lady Wei knew what he was going to do. He gathered up bamboo strips to weave them into small baskets, carriages, and figurines. The house was scattered with his creations. Old Lady Wei wondered why her son liked this hobby. She tried several times to persuade him to give it up, but it was to no avail. She could only let him do as he wished. It was strange that a scatterbrain like Xingguo spent hours on bamboo weaving. When Hong came to live with them, Old Lady Wei thought she might distract him from this hobby of his. But nothing changed.

"A woman will despise the man who is engaged in this kind of meaningless hobby," Old Lady once said to her son.

Xingguo only laughed. "How could that be? She fully supports me."

His answer was not what she had expected.

"Hong thinks this is art," Xingguo said, excited to tell his mother. "She told me she was impressed."

Old Lady Wei knew Hong often made flattering remarks to her son. She also knew that the woman was not only shrewd, but was sharp like a razor. Old Lady Wei confided in Auntie Zhang about her concerns, but the latter did not seem to be on the same page with her.

"So long as they are happy, you don't need to worry about what they do," Auntie Zhang said. "And it's good for her to hold your son in high esteem. Do you want to see them quarreling all day long?"

Old Lady Wei said that was not what she meant. "She holds him in great esteem because she hasn't yet gotten hold of him. If she gets hold of him some day, nobody knows how she will treat him."

Auntie Zhang could not help laughing. "Your son is a man, not a thing. Why did you use the expression 'get hold of'? I think you're overanxious. People around you will be unhappy because you're unhappy. If she is so cunning, why should she—"

Auntie Zhang stopped with a smile. Old Lady

Wei knew what she was going to say. She soon came to realize what Auntie Zhang was implying. A Shanghai *hukou* was not as highly sought after as before since people can earn money in many other places. What's more, Hong was not an ugly woman. Old Lady Wei could not reconcile herself to failure. She did not think her son was inferior to anyone else. If he had not been disabled from polio, he would have a child in high school by now.

When she chatted with Hong, Old Lady Wei asked her what Shangrao was like. She described it as a small town. There weren't as many high-rise buildings as in Shanghai. The streets were narrower and there weren't as many vehicles either.

Old Lady Wei was shocked. "You mean there are also vehicles?"

Hong was surprised by her question. "Mom, do Shanghai people think all other places are backwards?"

Old Lady Wei was so ashamed that she quickly and repeatedly said no.

"Shangrao is a prefectural town. Though it is less than half the size of Shanghai, its green environment and air quality are excellent," Hong explained. "The price of housing has been increasing in the past two years and the residential buildings downtown costs ten thousand yuan per square meter."

Old Lady Wei clucked her tongue in admiration. "It sounds better than Shanghai. More green environment, good air quality, and cheaper housing."

Hong smiled. "It can't compare to Shanghai. Shanghai is a beautiful city with the Bund, the Oriental Pearl TV Tower, and Jinmao Mansion. No other city is better than Shanghai."

She paused and then let out a sigh. "Shangrao and Shanghai are only different in the second character, but they are worlds apart."

Old Lady Wei stared at Hong for a while before letting out a sigh of her own. "There's not much difference. A lot of people still sleep on the streets in Shanghai. They can't eat in the fine restaurants on the Bund and in the Oriental Pearl TV Tower. Ordinary people live more or less the same life as before."

Hong was adept at knitting and it took her only a day to finish. She handed the knitted scarf to Old Lady Wei, who put on her bifocal glasses to check her work. When she was satisfied, she told her to give it to Xingguo.

"The scarf was your idea. You'd better give it to him yourself," Hong said.

"Who gives it to him makes no difference. It's not as though he will get any extra benefit if I give it to him."

Hong relented and brought the scarf to Xingguo.

"Mom, this is a beautiful scarf," Xingguo said jubilantly as he came down the stairs with the scarf around his neck a moment later. "Thank you very much."

Old Lady Wei knew her son well. An indifferent man like him would never express his gratitude in such an obvious way. It was no doubt Hong's doing.

"There's no need to thank me," Old Lady Wei abruptly responded. "I have never heard you say thank you to me since the day you were born. Is a scarf worth your thanks?"

Old Lady Wei brought Hong to the hairdresser. Hong's long hair was dry and dull. She wore it in a no-nonsense ponytail, which looked like a broom, and an old stiff whisky one at that. Old Lady Wei suggested she cut her ponytail for a bob. The hairdresser said the style of the bob suited the shape of her face.

"Isn't this a mushroom hairstyle?" Old Lady Wei said when the hairdresser finished his work.

The hairdresser laughed. "Granny, you're an expert. The Bob is the mushroom hairstyle, but a more refined and updated one."

Hong studied herself in the mirror and was satisfied with her new hairstyle.

"This auntie of yours looks at least five years younger," the hairdresser said to Old Lady Wei.

In Shanghai, a maid is called "auntie." Old Lady Wei could not help staring at Hong. Meanwhile, Hong concentrated on examining her bangs and probably did not hear what the hairdresser had said. Old Lady Wei asked the price and the answer was forty yuan.

Old Lady Wei sighed as she took out the money from her purse. "I can buy a lot of pork chops with this money,"

The hairdresser smiled. "You're getting a good deal in our shop. If you go to a beauty salon, the same haircut will cost you three times as much, and they may not even do a better job than us."

On their way home, Old Lady Wei passed by a market and wanted to buy some meat and vegetables. She asked Hong what she liked to eat. Hong said she had no personal preference.

"Then let's buy some pork chops," Old Lady Wei said jokingly.

"OK," Hong said, smiling sheepishly.

"Deep-fried pork chops are Xingguo's favorite. It's delicious, but it's high in cholesterol."

"It does no harm if you eat it occasionally."

The stallholder took out several pork chops and put them on the platform scale. "A little over one and half kilos. That will be twenty yuan."

Old Lady Wei started to take out her purse when Hong rushed to pay for it. She gave the stallholder twenty yuan and handed another twenty yuan to Old Lady Wei. "That's for my haircut."

Old Lady Wei was taken aback. "Why?"

"I'll pay for my haircut. It's not right for you to pay for it."

Hong took the pork chops and walked away. Old Lady Wei stalled for a while and then followed Hong. "Why did you do that? It doesn't make any difference whether you pay or I pay—"

"That's why it's the same if I pay," Hong said to Old Lady Wei while dodging her attempts at returning the money to her. "Mom, why don't you go back home first? I'll be along after I visit with some friends here."

Her friend Du Qin was over thirty years old and worked as a maid in the next lane. Hong often went to meet her when she was free so they could talk in their local dialect without holding back, especially when it came to weighty issues on their minds. Du Qin's employer was a lonely, eccentric old man without any children who was difficult to please. Du Qin often complained to Hong about the old man's peculiar behavior. Hong comforted her and suggested that she should leave his home and find a new employer if she was so unhappy. She could earn money anywhere she liked. Du Qin admired Hong by saying that the latter had fortune smiling down on her. The meat pie fell from the heaven and dropped onto her head.

This made Hong's lips curl into a smile. "Have you seen Xingguo's pockmarked face? It looks more like a pie covered in sesame instead of a meat pie."

Both of them burst out laughing.

Du Qin complimented her friend's new hairstyle. "Now you look like a real Shanghai girl. Old Lady Wei will want you to marry her son for sure."

"Things haven't even started to go that way yet,"

Hong said when Du Qin asked her when they would get married.

"But it's already been several months since you came to Shanghai."

"I'm afraid I may have a hard time ahead."

Du Qin could not contain her indignation. "That old woman is so full of herself. Her house is as small as a pigeon's and her son is a cripple. Why is she so arrogant?"

When she reached the entrance of their lane, Hong spotted Xingguo in an animated conversation with Xiaoying, a girl who owned a flour stall. Xiaoying became so excited that she patted her flour-covered hand on Xingguo's face, leaving two white palm traces. Xingguo laughed so hard that his gums showed. Hong hid herself in the corner and walked back home only after Xingguo went upstairs.

Old Lady Wei asked her son what had happened when she saw the two white palm traces on his face. Xingguo said he was stained with a little lime. Hong took a towel and wiped off the flour traces on his face.

"Thank you!" Xingguo said.

"You were not working on a construction site," Hong said softly as she wiped his face. "How could you be stained with lime?"

"I have no idea," Xingguo answered. "It's strange."

The next day, Xingguo suggested they go watch a morning show. Hong turned down his invitation with the excuse of having to wash the quilt cover.

"You can wash the quilt cover anytime," Xingguo said. "Why don't you postpone it until tomorrow?"

"The weatherman says it will be overcast tomorrow," She responded loudly on purpose.

Old Lady Wei came over. "Go to the movies. Today is a nice day."

"That's why I planned to wash the quilt cover," Hong said, and then turned to Xingguo. "We'll go to the movies when it rains."

Xingguo was unable to swallow his laugh. "Why should we go to the movies on a rainy day?"

Hong ignored him and took the detached quilt cover to the balcony. Old Lady Wei wanted to be nice to Hong and did not expect her kindness to be met with a mild rebuff. She felt her chest sink, blaming the little woman for this weird feeling. She looked at Xingguo suspiciously. "Did you quarrel with each other?"

"No, we didn't," he replied. "I'm a bit baffled myself."

While washing the quilt cover, Hong went over what had just happened. She was taking Du Qin's advice; don't act too submissively. Sometimes you should put on airs and get into a huff. That's the way to get along in a family. "You ought to know your position in their family. You are his wife instead of his maid. A maid should be submissive to her employer. A wife is different. From time to time, she should vent her frustrations to him and show her displeasure with her mother-in-law. That's how a wife should behave."

When she first heard this advice from Du Qin, Hong had burst out laughing. "I didn't expect that you to know so much."

Hong asked Xingguo to come to the balcony and help her wring out the quilt cover. "I'm not strong enough. I need your help."

"What's my reward?" Xingguo asked while they were wringing out the cover.

Hong gave him the evil eye. "Why should I reward you since this is your quilt cover?"

"This is Mom's quilt cover, and not mine," Xingguo said.

"Go and ask your mother to give you a reward then," Hong shot back.

Seeing that they were alone on the balcony, Xingguo, grinning hideously, went over and started to press his lips to her face.

Hong quickly dodged him. "No!"

Xingguo grabbed her waist with one hand and groped her breasts with the other.

"You devil!" Hong cursed.

A wicked smile tugged at the corner of Xingguo's mouth. Hong scooped up a wet pillow towel from the basin. She flung it at Xingguo and spattered him all over with water. When he could barely open his eyes, Hong clutched a lock of his hair and gave it a sharp pull. He let out a loud cry. Then and there, Hong whispered to him, "The weatherman says it'll rain tomorrow."

2

The neighborhood committee organized a day trip for sightseeing in Shanghai. Old Lady Wei signed up herself and Hong. The trip was eighty yuan each person, including lunch and an entrance ticket for the Oriental Pearl TV Tower. She asked Hong whether she wanted to go. It was a rhetorical question since she had already paid for the trip.

Since her arrival in Shanghai, Hong had never gone sightseeing except for a visit to Nanjing Road. Old Lady Wei did not think that was enough for a new visitor to Shanghai. Hong often wrote back home. It was only natural that her parents would ask her whether she had visited the Town God's Temple tourist spot, the Oriental Pearl TV Tower, and Jinmao Mansion. What a shame if she answered she had visited none of them during her six months' stay in Shanghai! Now that she had booked the day trip, she could visit all the tourist attractions in Shanghai in one day, even though she would only just get a quick glance of each one.

All the participants met at eight o'clock at the entrance of the residential area. Old Lady Wei turned down her son's request to go with them. "All the participants are women. It will be strange if a man joins us."

"If you really like to go, I'll give you my ticket." Hong said to Xingguo.

"He won't like to visit these places," Old Lady Wei said. "Only non-natives of Shanghai are interested."

As soon as she finished her sentence, Old Lady Wei knew instantly she had let her tongue slipped. She glanced at Hong's awkward look and tried to smooth over her embarrassment. "Well, the natives of Shanghai don't have many chances to visit these tourist attractions. Nowadays, non-natives fare much better than natives. All the rich people are non-natives."

Hong was carsick and felt like vomiting when the tour bus pulled away. Old Lady Wei asked the driver for a plastic bag. At that moment, Hong threw up all she had eaten for breakfast. She said she had a stomach ache. The two women sitting in front fanned their noses in obvious disgust.

At first, Old Lady Wei was annoyed at Hong for the inconvenience she had caused for her. But when she saw the behavior of the two women, she stood firmly by Hong. "Car sickness is common."

The two women responded by clicking their tongues. Mischievousness came over Old Lady Wei, and she swayed the plastic bag of vomit in front of their faces as soon as the driver slammed on the brakes. The two women let out a loud scream. "What's the matter with you?"

Old Lady Wei repressed her smile. "I'm sorry. I

didn't expect the sudden brake—"

They had meat filled soup dumplings for lunch at the Town God's Temple. Hong was not hungry. Old Lady Wei picked up some and put them in her bowl. "Have a little taste! The Town God's Temple is famous for these *xiaolong baozi*. You will regret it if you don't eat them while you're here."

Old Lady Wei poured more vinegar into her dish before continuing attempts to get Hong to eat. "Eating more vinegar will settle your stomach."

With some effort, Hong managed to eat two dumplings. Old Lady Wei went to the tour leader. "Hong doesn't feel well. We'll have to cut short our trip and go back home after lunch."

"Even if you cancel your afternoon tour, your tickets will not be refunded," the tour leader reminded her.

"I know," Old Lady Wei said. "What can I do when she is sick?"

They took the subway back home.

"Mom, I'm sorry for spoiling your fun," Hong apologized.

Old Lady Wei shook her head dismissively. "We can have a lot of fun in the future. Don't worry!"

It was the first time that Hong had taken the subway. Without holding the handrail tightly, she fell back several steps when the train suddenly started to move. Thanks to Old Lady Wei's timely grasp, she did not fall down. "Be careful!"

Hong patted her chest and smiled bashfully at Old Lady Wei.

When it was time to leave the station, Hong could not find her ticket. She searched every pocket, but it was nowhere to be found. Old Lady Wei paid three yuan to buy another ticket for her. Hong followed Old Lady Wei out of the station, her face flushed with embarrassment. Old Lady Wei noticed all this and her heart went out to Hong.

"The subway is not like the bus," Old Lady Wei explained, instead of admonishing her. "You should keep the ticket until you exit."

"The subway is like the railway," Hong mused.

"That's right. The subway is like the railway, but it's underground."

When they got back home, Old Lady Wei told Hong to lie in the bed. She boiled some water and prepared a hot water bottle for her. She cooked noodles and brought the steaming bowl to Hong. "I didn't put any meat in this for fear of upsetting your stomach. Help yourself to it."

Hong felt her heart warmed as she took the bowl of noodles. "Thank you, Mom."

Old Lady Wei sat on the side of the bed and looked at Hong questioningly. "Do you often have stomach aches?"

"My stomach hurts in the winter months and after eating spicy food."

"Have you seen the doctor?"

"No."

"You can't continue like this. You should go for a check up. Stomach aches may be a sign of serious problems. Don't take it so lightly."

Old Lady Wei acted swiftly and brought Hong to the hospital the next day for an endoscopy. The diagnosis was that she had a mild ulcer caused by helicobacter pylori, a kind of bacteria.

"The bacteria are contagious," the doctor explained. "Chinese people are likely to contract this disease because we don't like to serve the meal individually. It's nothing serious, but you have to take medication."

The doctor prescribed three medicines for half

a month.

At supper, Old Lady Wei put a spoon in every plate. "We should learn from the foreigners. Let's use these serving spoons to get food into our own bowls."

Xingguo did not want to go to the trouble with the serving spoons and insisted on using his chopsticks to pick food directly from the plates. Old Lady Wei intercepted his chopsticks with her own chopsticks. "We are going to use serving spoons. Being careful will do all of us good."

Hong remained silent. She used the serving spoons to get some bok choy and finished her meal quickly. She thought Old Lady Wei was afraid that she might transmit her disease to them. When she heard the doctor say that the bacteria in her stomach had surpassed the normal standard, a sinking feeling came over her. It was frightening to learn there were bacteria in her stomach. The thought depressed her. When she came out of the kitchen after she washed the bowls and plates, she saw Old Lady Wei talking softly with Xingguo. The latter lifted his head and gave her a quick glance. Hong suspected that they were talking about her.

Her guess was right. A few minutes later Old Lady

Wei washed her feet and went to bed. Only she and Xingguo stayed in the living room. As usual, Xingguo pushed up against her and touched her all over, but avoided kissing her. Hong gave a silent snort and pushed him away. "I'm tired. I want to go to sleep."

"It's still early," Xingguo insisted. "You're not an old woman."

"If I'm not an old woman, do you think I'm still a young girl?" Hong said sulkily.

Xingguo grinned cheekily. He showed her the knickknack he had woven during the day—a sedan made with very thin bamboo chips. On the back of the painted sedan, there was a lifelike logo of Mercedes-Benz. Hong wanted to ignore him at first, but she was curious about his handiwork. She took it from him. "What skillful hands you have!"

"Of course," Xingguo said with a complacent smile. "Your husband is a deft hand."

Hong let off some invisible steam through her nose. "My husband? I don't dare have such expectations."

"Well, if I'm not your husband, do you think I'm somebody else's husband?" Xingguo countered.

"Perhaps sooner or later," Hong muttered.

Xingguo grinned roguishly and tried to put his hand on her shoulder. She wrinkled her brow and stepped aside. He tried again and she moved again. After several rounds of this, Xingguo complained. "How is it you're as slippery as a fish?"

Old Lady Wei could not fall asleep so she heard their conversation while she was lying in her bed. Judging from Hong's attitude, Old Lady Wei knew that she was being overly paranoid about her stomach condition, which wasn't a serious one at all. Old Lady Wei gave a huge yawn. Then she heard Xingguo utter "ouch." He was obviously in a great deal of pain. She heard him yell out, "My hand is broken, broken—"

Then she heard Hong's muffled voice. "Don't you dare do it again—"

This was followed by scurrying footsteps. Probably one was running from the other. The staircase was squeaking. Then she heard them laughing merrily. Old Lady Wei knew they were flirting with each other. She thought: men are born contemptible wretches. They are always obedient when they get scoldings and beatings from their little women.

She recalled the wonderful days she had spent with her late husband when she was young. Though it had been dozens of years, she could still see the scenes with her eyes from time to time. Xingguo took after his father and their noses were exactly alike. It is said a son has a good fortune if he takes after his mother. If he had looked like her, he would not have suffered so much. What lousy luck! Her son contracted the damned disease and became a cripple before the age of five. Her husband died of an injury at work when she was about thirty years old. She was left a lonely widow with a disabled son. She was so desperate that she even thought of ending her wretched life. She weathered many bitter years with a simple thought: "I'll live as everybody else does." So, a solitary widow and her fatherless son held out to now. The bitter bleeding had stopped and a scab had formed over the wound. Their scarred skin was stronger than others. Old Lady Wei did not ask for much. She only wished that her son would marry a decent woman and have a child and they would live a quiet and peaceful life.

Auntie Zhang came several times for Old Lady Wei's response.

"I don't want to rush," Old Lady Wei said. "Let's wait and see."

"Your Xingguo is well over 40!" Auntie Zhang exclaimed.

"Haste makes waste. He's selecting a wife instead of a cabbage. It will never be too prudent to enter into a marriage."

"I know a marriage is an important matter. But no matter how important a matter is, you have to make a decision sooner or later. I think Hong is a good girl."

Old Lady Wei gave her a faint smile. She knew very well that Hong went to Auntie Zhang's home very often. She helped Auntie Zhang with all kinds of household chores; washing clothes, mopping the floor, and cooking meals. She even spent her own wage buying snacks for Auntie Zhang. Old Lady Wei did not think Hong had done anything inappropriate. If she were in her place, she would be doing the same. It was understandable. It was better for her son to find a calculating wife. Simple-minded as her son was, he needed the support of a capable wife. Old Lady Wei tried to convince herself of this. It was not easy to find a good wife in the world now. She hoped that she could give an answer soon. All of them would be relieved, including her.

It was getting quiet outside. They must have gone to sleep. Old Lady Wei draped a jacket over her shoulders and went out of her bedroom. The cloth screen of the small room was not drawn too closed. The lamplight came out through the slit. She halted and looked inside only to see Hong sitting on the bed writing a letter. The quilt was soft, so she put a desk calendar on it. Knitting her brows, she wrote slowly and was scrupulous about every stroke. The paper was half filled with closely written characters. Her writing posture was strange because she held the pen the way people held a writing brush. With her middle finger propping the shaft, she wrote with great effort. Sweat was beading her forehead. It was the first time that Old Lady Wei had seen her writing a letter. The way she wrote a letter was so different from the way she did housework. Old Lady Wei's curiosity was aroused. Light from the lamp fell in a shade of warm color on her head. Her long hair hung over half of her face.

Old Lady Wei stared at her for a while. She was about to leave when her elbow accidentally knocked on the wall. Hong heard the thump and raised her head.

The two women looked at each other silently.

It was Hong who spoke first. "Mom...I'm...I'm almost done. I'll turn off the light right away."

She quickly put the letter aside and lay down in the bed while reaching out to turn off the desk lamp.

Old Lady Wei knew that Hong had misunderstood. She waved her hand. "Go ahead with your writing. I was just going to the bathroom."

When she came out of the bathroom, she saw the screen drawn closed completely. The desk lamp was turned off and it was pitch black. Hong's small room was so quiet. It seemed that she had fallen asleep. Old Lady Wei was taken aback and stood at the door for a few seconds. A wave of regret washed over her as she found her way back to her bedroom. If Hong became her daughter-in-law, she would tell her son to treat her kindly.

On New Year's Day Xingguo bought a cashmere cardigan for his mother. Its original price was two thousand yuan and he got it at a discount of forty percent. Hong helped her put it on. Old Lady Wei admired herself in the mirror.

"I'm an old woman. Why should you spend money on me?" She gushed even though she was please with her son's gift.

"Who says an old woman should not dress fashionably?" Xingguo teased. "And your son is not poor anymore."

Old Lady Wei was stunned by his remark. It reminded her that her son had not asked her for money in the past few weeks. However, they still went to the movie theatre for morning shows. They went window-shopping in Huaihai Road twice. They even visited Jinjiang Amusement Park last week. His monthly wage and bonus were still in her drawer. Where did he get the money?

Old Lady Wei became worried. She was afraid that her son had been gambling day and night like those rascals at the entrance of the lane. That would be terrible. If anything goes wrong, he would lose all his fortune. Xingguo was always a trouble-maker. When he was in junior high school, he and his mischievous classmates stole metal scraps from a factory and sold them to the salvage station. While his classmates were quick in movement, his lame leg prevented him from running away. As a result, he got caught by the factory's gatekeeper. Old Lady Wei was both angry and scared. She hung her son from the roof beam and whipped him soundly with a belt. She wiped her tears while giving him a hard whipping. She had rather beat him to death than see him go astray. It would save her a lot of worries. Fortunately, with her diligence and guidance her son reined in before he had gone too far.

At the thought of this, Old Lady Wei broke out in a cold sweat. She found it inconvenient to ask her son in Hong's presence. As soon as Hong went out to the balcony to bring in the laundry, she asked her son with if he had a conscience. Hong came to Shanghai to marry a decent husband. If Xingguo were acting shamefully, even an ugly woman won't accept him, to say nothing of a girl from Shangrao. Her voice quivered when she spoke to him. To her surprise, her son bellowed with laughter. "Mom, it's only your imagination. Your lecture is wasted on me."

Xingguo pulled out a small suitcase from under the bed. He opened it to show a full load of knickknacks. He turned over the suitcase and all the bamboo-made carriages, figurines, and animals fell noisily onto the floor.

"Do you know one can make money with one's craftsmanship?" Xingguo said proudly.

He told his mother that Hong had opened

an online shop selling these knickknacks. In the beginning, they intended to give it a try. They had not expected people to place any orders. The first customers commented that they admired the fine craftsmanship of his work, but was dissatisfied with their simple packing. Acting on their advice, Hong bought scarlet cardboard and made small boxes by herself. She put each piece of his handiwork in a red box and tied it with a golden ribbon. Each box was decorated with the Chinese character for happiness. Nowadays people liked to play games at weddings. Hong believed that their products would be ideal prizes for the games—inexpensive but exquisite. The results proved that Hong's judgment was right. The repackaged articles sold much better. They sold at least a dozen of them each week.

"If business is brisk like this, there won't be enough in stock. I have to make more. Mom, you always complain that my work wasn't even decent. You even told me to throw them away. Fortunately, Hong is a girl of foresight—" Xingguo said excitedly, emitting saliva in all directions.

Hong came out of the kitchen and heard what Xingguo was saying. She had to cut in. "I just wanted to give it a try. I didn't expect it to work. It was sheer luck on my part—just like a blind cat stumbling upon a dead rat."

"What counts is your husband's superb craftsmanship," Xingguo added.

Hong darted a scornful look at him. "Don't toot your own horn."

At first, Old Lady Wei was relieved. But when she saw the two of them act in such a tacit way, she could not refrain from feeling sadly envious. "Doing business is a good choice, but you must be prepared for risks. Nobody can guarantee your profits."

"There won't be any risks," Xingguo said. "Ours is an intellectual investment and no capital is required."

"Is that true? Is cardboard not capital?" Old Lady Wei said scornfully. "Is labor not capital? Are your brain cells not capital? Are those bamboo chips not capital?"

Xingguo stamped his foot. "Oh, you're being nitpicky!"

Old Lady Wei deliberately warned them against bad luck. After making her disheartening remark, she walked to the bathroom contentedly. If anything, she was delighted from the bottom of her heart. Without resorting to stealing or robbery, her son made money by sitting at home. Fancy those people buying those small worthless articles! What is the world coming? Old Lady Wei regretted having forgotten to ask them how much they had earned. She did not think their earnings were meager. They watched movies and went window-shopping after all. Sometimes they even went to a café or a restaurant. One must spend money when dating. Dating expenses give people the greatest pleasure. Her son was already over forty and enjoys this kind of pleasure twenty years later than other men. Anyway, he's enjoying it now. Old Lady Wei felt light and easy.

"How did you come up with the idea of selling online?" Old Lady Wei asked Hong.

"A-mei on the third floor taught me," Hong answered.

A-mei worked at the cosmetics counter in a department store. When the manufacturers launch promotions, they hand out their trial products. A-mei often hides these trial products and tells customers that all of them have been given. Then she sells them online. This has become an open secret in the cosmetics industry. Old Lady Wei dislikes her. She is disgusted at her dyed multi-colored hair and painted black nails. "How can she be a good teacher when she herself is so coy?"

Hong told Old Lady Wei that she started a business by renting her online shop. With the expansion of her business, she registered a shop online. "There're many online shops like this and we face strong competition from others. Fortunately, Xingguo's superb craftsmanship has enabled us to survive."

Xingguo darted her a wicked look. "So you've come to admit I'm talented."

Xingguo had suggested they dine out tonight. "To celebrate your son making a fortune."

Old Lady Wei rejected his proposal. "We'd better live frugally. Anyway, dining out is not sanitary. It'll be cheaper and cleaner to eat at home and cooking a few more dishes."

"It matters little to you because you're not the cook," Xingguo muttered.

His remark grated on his mother. Old Lady Wei thought her son was already taking Hong's side even though they were not yet married.

"I can cook, too," Old Lady Wei said coldly. "I'll

do the cooking. She can take a break."

While mother and son were still arguing, Hong hurried out to the market. She started to prepare dinner immediately after she got back. The dining table was filled with delicious delicacies, such as fried hairtail, sweet and sour spareribs, broccoli in oyster sauce, and shredded dried tofu with salted vegetable. All these were Old Lady Wei's favorite dishes. Xingguo picked up his chopsticks and helped himself. He praised Hong for her cooking. "My wife's culinary skill is remarkable."

The chicken soup was stewed on the cooking range. Hong served a bowl to Old Lady Wei. "Mom, please taste it and tell me whether it's salty."

Old Lady Wei took a spoonful of the soup. "It's OK."

"I put some dried scallops in the soup," Hong said. "It seems to smell a bit pungent."

Old Lady Wei had taught her to soak dried scallops in yellow rice wine for a while and then shred them before putting them into the soup. "You should not throw the dried scallops directly into the soup. Do you think they are heads of garlic?"

There was a sting in her remark, but Hong only

smiled. "Yes, you're right. I've just learned another cooking trick from you, Mom."

In private Old Lady Wei asked her son how much he had earned. Xingguo deliberately kept her mother in suspense. "Not a small sum." But when pressed by his mother for an answer, Xingguo told her that it depended on the quality of his work and most of the time he earned one to two hundred yuan.

The number shocked Old Lady Wei. "Do you mean each piece?"

"Of course each piece," Xingguo answered, a bit annoyed. "Do you think it's a whole sack of them? Do you think they are sold to the salvage station? These are works of art. Mom, your son is an artist!"

Old Lady Wei was genuinely speechless. One piece costs one to two hundred yuan. What a lot of money they can earn if they sell a dozen pieces each week? Old Lady Wei could not help feeling that she was behind the times. Although she has lived in Shanghai all her life, she never learned to make money this way. Hong had been in Shanghai for only a few months and has mastered this trick of turning useless knickknacks into precious handicrafts. She did not expect that her son would become such a money tree. At the thought of this, she burst into laughter. Feeling both proud and worried, she shared this secret with Auntie Zhang. The latter took the opportunity to speak highly of Hong. "What a smart girl she is! You've acquired a real treasure."

Old Lady Wei said, "What I fear most is that she is too smart. You see, they made a fortune without my knowledge."

"It's better to keep out of their daily activities," Auntie Zhang said.

Old Lady Wei thought it over. "Xingguo is a careless blockhead. I'm afraid he is no match for her."

Auntie Zhang tried to persuade her. "Since both of them are so willing to play their roles, you don't need to worry about their petty matters. What's more, without Hong's discerning eyes, you would still be treating your precious son like a worthless stone. As an entrance guard, how much does he earn? Everything has changed now. As a moonlighter, his income has surpassed that of a white-collar worker. It shows that every match is predestined in the world. Your son probably hasn't gotten married yet because he was waiting for her. It's destiny."

Old Lady Wei believed in fate all the more in her

old age. Auntie Zhang's remark struck a chord in her heart. All in all, there's no absolute standard to judge a wife-to-be. She is a good choice if only she treats Xingguo well. Now that he was fond of Hong, Old Lady Wei should only consider her son's interests. What else does she want? Old Lady Wei heaved a sigh of relief despite the tinge of regret when she spoke to Auntie Zhang. "If only I had known earlier that Xingguo has such a skill, I would have looked for a girl in Shanghai for him to marry. Why should I go to the trouble of finding his partner from so far away?"

Auntie Zhang shook her head. "You're already an old woman. Why are you still so fussy about such things?"

Hong was pregnant. She felt sick and threw up for a few days. People thought she had a stomach ache again. Xingguo accompanied her to the hospital for a check up.

After they came back home, Xingguo looked at Old Lady Wei with an excited gleam in his eyes. "Mom, she's pregnant."

Old Lady Wei's heart beat wildly with joy. But on the exterior she pretended to be calm and put on a stern expression. "Look, you're still kids without getting married. Now you're making a mess of things."

When she glanced at Hong, she was blushing with shame. Old Lady Wei tried not to disgrace her too much. "Come, come, what's done cannot be undone."

Filled with joy, Old Lady Wei banged her fist on her son. "What a nuisance! You've gotten into trouble!"

One piece of good fortune after another smiled on them. A few days later, news came that their old house was going to be torn down. It was no rumor anymore because the neighborhood committee had put up a notice. The resettlement project was expected to begin in April next year and all the residents were requested to support their work. Old Lady Wei made a careful calculation: if her son gets married before the end of the year, there will be two households with three registered residents. They will be allotted a dozen more square meters of housing. The extra housing will cost tens of thousands of yuan. Fortune is on their side. The timing is just right. Good things always come in pairs.

There was not enough time to visit Hong's

parents in Jiangxi. Old Lady Wei planned to discuss with them about the marriage over the phone or by letter. People in Jiangxi have their customs. Even if time is critical, she should show respect to their customs. She refused to give them the impression that Shanghai people were unrefined.

"Is it the custom to deliver betrothal gifts in your hometown?" Old Lady Wei asked Hong. "It's not necessary," Hong said. "My parents won't set great importance to this. What they value most is that I'll live a happy life."

Old Lady Wei thought Hong was being polite. She decided to give them some gifts to express her gratitude. In addition, she had to prepare some gold and silver jewelry.

Old Lady Wei brought Hong to the jeweler's shop. She selected a pure gold wrist chain. She also bought a diamond ring. Though the ring core was made of crushed diamonds, the inexpensive ring still flashed brilliantly. Hong's fingers were fat and white, almost the size of a man's. The salesman praised Hong for her naturally rich lady's hands and said they would bring good fortune to her family. Old Lady Wei thought she was not sure whether she would bring them good fortune, but she knew very well that the ring had cost her a great fortune. The family's monthly expenditure increased, but she still felt happy. At the age of seventy, she finally got the chance to buy jewelry for her future daughter-in-law.

Xingguo's marriage to Hong became household news in the lane. Old Lady Wei was not afraid of the idle gossip that her lame son was going to marry a maid coming from a distant place. It doesn't matter. Every family can choose the way they want to live. As the old saying goes, only the wearer knows where the shoe pinches. Who can predict what will happen in the future? Even if a physically abled man marries a Shanghai girl, who can ensure that they will live together to a ripe old age? Old Lady Wei has endured untold sufferings. She knows very well that what matters most on earth is these two words—"real benefit." When Xingguo's father died, Old Lady Wei was ready to risk everything in order to get a better pension for her bereaved family. Saving face was not as important as feeding herself and her son. If she had hesitated at that time, she and her son would not have survived—all this happened decades ago. What is past is past. She didn't need to look back.

Old Lady Wei asked Hong to burn incense and offer sacrifices to Xingguo's late father. The photo of the deceased was taken out from the drawer, cleaned, and put on the chest of drawers. Hong burned a joss stick and bowed three times.

"This is your daughter-in-law," Old Lady Wei said. "She is with child now. I hope you'll bless and protect them."

"Dad," Hong said with the utmost respect to the photo.

Old Lady Wei felt a lump in her throat and tried her best to hold back tears.

Old Lady Wei wanted to reduce Hong's burden of household chores. Hong insisted on doing housework with the excuse that more activity would be good for a pregnant woman.

"After you give birth to a baby, you'll have a lot of activity," Old Lady Wei said. "Now is the time for you to rest."

As Hong's small room faced north and was cold and damp, Old Lady Wei urged her to move into the big bedroom, spacious and sunny. Xingguo complained that his mother was biased toward her daughter-in-law.

"OK, starting from today, you'll sleep in the small room and I'll climb up to the attic," Old Lady Wei shot back bluntly.

Old Lady Wei did not allow Xingguo to make bamboo knickknacks anymore, for fear that Hong might inhale sawdust and develop a cough. "A pregnant woman can't take any medication. She will suffer a lot if she becomes sick."

In their leisure time, Old Lady Wei taught Hong how to speak the Shanghai dialect. When they shelled green soya beans in the kitchen, Old Lady Wei corrected her mouth movement and pronunciation. In China, the Shanghai dialect is one of the easiest dialects to understand and learn. However, it is very difficult to master authentic Shanghainese. This was because the Shanghai dialect is a branch of learning, both extensive and profound. You can compare it to the tea after several refills of boiling water. The light green water is so crystal-clear that you can see the reflection of a human figure. The tea leaves settle steadily at the bottom of the teacup, solid and clean.

Old Lady Wei advised Hong against speaking prematurely. "You'd better listen more. The more you are versed in the dialectal environment, the more naturally you can speak Shanghainese. The authentic Shanghai dialect is like a cracked hickory and listeners will enjoy its relaxed and crisp tone. When you listen to pidgin Shanghainese, you'll feel as though you're looking at a man dressed in a Western suit wearing a pair of sneakers.

"Mom, Shanghainese sounds like Japanese," Hong said.

"Really? I don't think so. The Japanese language is not as pleasant to the ear as Shanghainese."

"I think the pronunciation of 'have a meal' in Shanghainese is similar to that in the Shangrao dialect. Mom, please listen to my Shangrao dialect—" she said "have a meal" in the Shangrao dialect. "Am I right?"

Old Lady Wei agreed with her. "That explains why Shanghai and Shangrao are different only in one syllable."

Hong offered to teach Old Lady Wei the Shangrao dialect. Old Lady Wei quickly shook her head. "I'm an old woman. My brain has become rusty and I have a poor memory."

Hong would not listen to her. "How can it be? From now on, you teach me Shanghainese. I'll teach you the Shangrao dialect. Let's learn from each other."

Hong's persistence reminded Old Lady Wei of a spoiled child who spoke with a twang. Old Lady Wei thought her coyness bewitched Xingguo so effectively that she even conceived a baby.

Old Lady Wei shook her head with a sweet smile and patted Hong lightly on the head. They had never been this intimate with each other before. Hong almost moved her head to dodge as a conditioned reflex, but she did her best to restrain herself, thus, receiving a sign of affection from her future mother-in-law. Old Lady Wei's affectionate pat was a milestone-like significance. It was an epoch-making event. Hong tried every means to look natural, but something in her heart spilled upward, one flow after another, straight to her head. Her cheeks and then her eyes reddened. Her blushes rippled slowly to make her warm all over.

In addition to Shanghainese, Old Lady Wei showed Hong how to make up and dress herself. She bought *ELLE* and some other popular fashion magazines and used them as Hong's textbooks. It's much more difficult to imitate the models' ways of organizing their different pieces of clothing and arranging their hairstyles than to learn Shanghainese. It depended on one's innate ability and wisdom instead of mechanical copying. Old Lady Wei devoted herself heart and soul to training Hong to be a Shanghainese wife. As an old woman, she did not go in for ostentation out of vanity. She did all this simply for the sake of her son. Her son was just reaching middle age and still had a long way to go. Shanghai is a place difficult to describe in a few words. Sometimes it was kind and all encompassing; sometimes it was arrogant and unapproachable. Some firmly established prejudice was deep-rooted just like an anchor secured at the bottom of the sea. Shanghai people set great value by "face-saving." Just like the malt wrapping of a candy, it was not necessary, but the candy will look unrefined without it. Though "face-saving" was considered an additional ornament, Old Lady Wei won't feel at ease until her son's face is saved. In the last analysis, it is not only about "face-saving"; it also involves "dignity" or "self-esteem."

Old Lady Wei's self-esteem had been in a state of dormancy for decades. Her often silent and restrained self-esteem is slowly reviving like a dormant snake. Spring has finally come and she felt nice and warm.

Old Lady Wei was a quiet person and now is becoming talkative. She talks at length about the days she has spent in the past decades. Her true stories are as profound as a diary. Hong seemed to smell the fragrance of paper when Old Lady Wei turns over the pages of her "diary." Whether it is written in detail or in brief depends on Old Lady Wei's mood. Both delightful and sad stories unfold from the near to the distant. With the progress of her story telling, those almost forgotten years in her faint memory gradually emerged and became distinct just like photos being developed in the darkroom.

Hong was a good listener. The "days" spent with Old Lady Wei in Shanghai are not what she had imagined before. She had come to know what "spending days" meant. Hong thought before that the "days" of Shanghai were as brilliant as those shop windows. It seemed to her now the "days" are down to the earth. Removing their brilliant appearance, the "days" of Shanghai were brown. Shanghai's dark color and heavy texture make people hold their breath and become speechless. When you taste the "days" of Shanghai for the first time, you'll find them bitter and astringent. They will gradually turn fragrant and sweet. You'll enjoy a sweet life only after you experience a bitter life. Bitterness remains at the root of your tongue and sweetness originates from the bottom of your heart. Bitterness is the precursor of sweetness. There is no sweetness without bitterness—this is universal truth.

The two women basked in the sunshine in the courtyard, working together to wind the wool into a ball. The winter sunlight fell on their faces, presenting a picturesque view of beauty and tenderness.

It was a sunny day when they went to apply for a marriage registration. Xingguo and Hong left early. Old Lady Wei urged them to come back home as soon as they finished their registration. A pregnant woman should not strain herself. Old Lady Wei had made a reservation at a nearby restaurant that was recently opened for dinner.

Old Lady Wei tidied up the house and went out to empty the garbage. Only a few steps away from her house, she stepped on a banana peel at the corner and almost slipped and fell. Her garbage bag slipped from her hand and dropped on the ground.

"Damn it!" Old Lady Wei cursed.

She was about to pick up the bag when she saw

something coming out of the garbage bag—a rolled-up sanitary napkin. The loosened napkin was covered with a dark red bloodstain.

Old Lady Wei was so shocked that she cursed to herself. She stopped and turned the garbage bag inside out. She found another two dirty sanitary napkins. Old Lady Wei stood still and examined them carefully. Her heart sank. Slowly she picked them up.

Xingguo received his mother's call at the Bureau of Civil Affairs.

"Have you got your marriage certificate?"

"Not yet. We're having a photo taken now. What's wrong?"

"That's good—Withdraw your application and come back home right away!" Old Lady Wei uttered these words and hung up the telephone.

3

Hong did the packing. She put her blouses, jackets, trousers, and shoes into the suitcase. She hung her head, but was quick in motion. Standing to one side, Xingguo watched her. Both of them kept silent. Old

Lady Wei had gone out for a walk. Before she left, she told her son to accompany Hong to the bus stop. For the sake of their special relationship, he should see her off. Xingguo pouted his lips like a child. Old Lady Wei was aware of his unwillingness. She knew her son was reluctant to let the little woman go. Old Lady Wei pretended not to see his facial expression. If she didn't have a sense of propriety in handling this matter, she won't be a qualified mother. She purposely walked out without saying good-bye to them.

After she finished packing, Hong cast her eyes at Xingguo. She looked at him the way a pet cat looked at its owner. Her eyes brimmed with tears. She knew very well it was her final attempt and she did not think it would be successful. As expected, Xingguo avoided her eyes and picked up her suitcase. "Let's go."

Hong followed Xingguo to the bus stop. It was already past eight o'clock in the evening. That was Old Lady Wei's plan, because there won't be many neighbors in the lane at night, which would help to avoid further embarrassment. Xingguo gave a dry cough and touched his nose in a very unnatural manner.

"Why should I make things difficult for him?"

Hong said to herself.

She moved forward and took her suitcase from him. "Thank you for seeing me off. You can go back home."

"OK," Xingguo said, but he did not move his feet.

Hong sat down on the long bench and put the suitcase on her lap. She turned her eyes to the direction of arriving buses. Xingguo stood there in a daze for a few seconds.

"Actually—" he started to say, but shut his mouth as soon as he uttered the word.

Hong pretended not to hear him. What a useless person he was. She was so angry with herself for failing to get hold of such a man. Her eyes welled with tears of embarrassment.

"Time for you to go back home," she told him.

"I won't leave until you get on the bus."

"You'd better leave. If you stay here, I'll feel ill at ease."

Seeing that she had given the signal for him to leave, Xingguo walked away reluctantly. Due to both lameness and hesitation, he moved his feet with difficulty. It took a long time for him to make a turn and disappear. Hong turned her head and looked at her watch. It was almost nine o'clock. Only a few passengers were waiting at the bus stop. The dim street lamps made them look like ghosts.

Instead of waiting for the bus, Hong went to Du Qin's home. Her employer had gone to sleep. She was watching TV. She turned down the volume almost to mute as if she were a thief. She said the old man forbade her to watch TV alone in order to save electricity.

She was shocked to see Hong carrying a suitcase. "Did they find out your secret?"

Hong nodded her head and sat down on the sofa.

It was Du Qin's idea for Hong to feign pregnancy. "All is ready except is the most crucial part. I'll support you with all I have," she had said. "Old Lady Wei is an old woman. Nothing will please her more than having a grandson. If she is pleased, your marriage will be certain."

Hong had hesitated. "How can I give birth to a baby if I'm not pregnant?"

Du Qin chided her for being stupid. "One gives birth to a baby only after ten months of pregnancy. Anything can happen during that time. So long as you obtain the marriage certificate, it will be too late for her to undo what is done."

Hong thought Du Qing was right. She was no longer a virgin. Although her youth wasn't worth much, she was still a woman. Her marriage can't drag anymore. She would have to make a last effort. If she were successful, she would achieve her goal of turning herself from a Shangrao girl into a Shanghai woman. If she lost this gamble, she'd go back to her hometown and marry a native Shangrao man.

Du Qin couldn't shake her terribly guilty conscience. "If I had known what would happen, I would never have put forward such a lousy idea."

Hong waved her hand. "It's nothing serious. Life still goes on and the Earth is still turning." She decided not to go back to Shangrao right now. Instead, she would stay for a few more days to see what would happen. Du Qin knew what she meant: if she stayed here, there might still be hope. If she left Shanghai, that meant she'd given up hope completely.

The two women squeezed into the single bed. For fear of waking up the old man, they whispered to each other.

"My parents are overjoyed with my success,"

Hong said. "If they find out, I wonder how disappointed they will be."

"Then don't tell them."

"You can keep the matter secret for a period of time, but you can't keep it secret all your life. They will learn about it sooner or later."

"Guard your secret as long as possible. You haven't been driven to desperation yet."

Hong remained silent for a while. "Knowing that I deceived her like that, the old woman will really hate me."

"Being a woman, she will understand your situation when she no longer burns with hate." Hong sighed. "Not all women see eye to eye. I'm afraid she won't understand my situation."

Du Qin began to talk about herself. Her employer was diagnosed with uraemia and his disease was deteriorating. The doctor said he needed a kidney transplant.

"Kidneys are vital for any human being," Du Qin explained. "Who will donate a kidney to him for no reason? The head of the neighborhood committee had a talk with me and tried to persuade me into staying over the Spring Festival. She praised me for my good temper and proven capability. If I leave now, it will be impossible for them to find a substitute maid to look after such a fussy old man. I don't buy her unctuous praise. I will go back to my hometown to for the Spring Festival. I haven't returned home for several years."

"He is a pitiable old man without any children," Hong said.

"There is many more like him. Aren't we pitiable? Even the Almighty Heaven is unable to show pity on everyone," Du Qin said. "I thought I might benefit from your association with native Shanghai people. Now my dream has been shattered. We are still native Jiangxi people."

Hong gave a deep sigh, "I have an unhappy lot in life."

Du Qin heaved her own heavy sigh. "Me, too."

Hong did not sleep a wink that night. The bed was too small for them to turn over. But Du Qin managed to sleep soundly and even snored gently. Her husband worked at the construction site. The couple endured with dogged will and did not go back to their hometown for several years. Their daughter was reaching school age. As soon as she was born, her maternal grandparents looked after her daughter. Their daughter only met them—her own parents—several times. Her husband worked so hard that he was promoted to the rank of a foreman. What's more, his wage was doubled. So, their good mood was doubled, too. That's why the couple was prepared to go back home during the Spring Festival. They planned to bring their daughter to Shanghai after the Spring Festival. Though the rent was high in Shanghai, they were able to rent a small house. It was worth it to live together with their daughter. Du Qin told Hong that her daughter's pet name was "Crescent Moon" because an eyebrow-shaped moon, pretty and charming, appeared in mid-air when she was born. "Crescent Moon is going to be seven next year. She appears in my dream every night."

Hong glanced at Du Qin and saw a beam on her face. She must be dreaming of her daughter.

On her way to the park for her morning exercise, Old Lady Wei ran into Hong at the entrance of the lane. The little woman smiled and acknowledged her, "Mom."

Old Lady Wei was taken aback as if she had seen a ghost. "Didn't you leave?"

Hong did not reply right directly. "The sky is murky grey. It looks like rain."

Old Lady Wei ignored her and went on her way.

Before she entered the door of her apartment after her workout, Old Lady Wei caught a delicious smell of food. She saw Hong frying an egg in the kitchen. Xingguo was having his breakfast. Hong probably bought a plate of fried dumplings. Old Lady Wei stood there staring blankly for a few seconds.

Seeing his mother come in, Xingguo ducked his head and ate his breakfast. Hong greeted Old Lady Wei cordially. "Mom, come and have some fried dumplings. It's delicious."

Old Lady Wei darted her eyes from her son to Hong. She gave a silent snort. When she came out of the bathroom, she saw Hong cleaning the gas range.

Xingguo had finished his breakfast. "I'm going to work."

Hong took out an umbrella from the drawer and gave it to him. "It looks like rain. Bring an umbrella with you."

Xingguo hesitated for a while before taking it.

"What do you want to eat for supper?" Hong asked him. "How about sweet and sour pork ribs?"

Xingguo did not dare to answer her. He uttered a few words to himself while pushing open the door and going out. Old Lady Wei stood by observing Hong's behavior. She thought this little woman was shameless. She watched patiently.

"It's time for you to go," she said after Hong finished cleaning the gas range.

"Mom," Hong said her name and began to say something when Old Lady Wei waved her hand to stop her from talking.

"It's no use offering an explanation," Old Lady Wei said. "Go away! Don't come back again."

Hong pursed her lips and tears streamed down her cheeks. "Mom—I know I was wrong. Would you please forgive me and give me another chance? I promise you that I'll be nice to you and Xingguo all my life."

Old Lady Wei shook her head. "You don't need to be nice to us. If only you could live a good life!"

Hong was flooded with tears. "Mom, I admit I had selfish motives. I only aspired to attach myself to phoenixes. But I had no ill intention. I wanted to get married earlier so that I could wait upon you, a venerable old lady—"

Old Lady Wei cut her short. "I'm flattered. I don't have the happy luck to be cared for by you. Don't say that 'you aspired to attach yourself to phoenixes.' We dare not aspire to such an honor. My son Xingguo is a blockhead and you are a phoenix. He doesn't make a good match for you."

All of a sudden, Old Lady Wei recalled the remarks made by Auntie Zhang the other day: "Without her discerning eyes, you are still treating your precious son like a worthless stone. Your son probably hasn't gotten married because he's waiting for her. It's destiny."

She felt torn by conflicting emotions. Oh, what a pity! Still wearing a cold look, she turned around and stood with her back facing Hong.

Hong stood against the wall and absentmindedly scratched it with her fingers. She cast her red-ringed eyes at the floor. She kept silent and stood still. Old Lady Wei waited for some time and did not see Hong move her feet. She felt ill at ease. She could not drive her away with a broom for fear that her neighbors might see them. She couldn't lose face in front of them. How could they remain at a deadlock like this? They had a tacit contest against each other. The room was so quiet that the ticking of the wall clock was audible. Every second was a torment to them.

Old Lady Wei sat down and turned on the television. Hong started moving, too. She turned about and fetched the mop. Old Lady Wei was perplexed when she saw what Hong was doing. She was mopping the floor meticulously.

"Mom, could you please lift your feet?" She asked.

Old Lady Wei did not know whether she should lift her feet. She simply stood up and moved to the kitchen to prepare food. A moment later Hong came in. She put a small stool beside Old Lady Wei and sat down giving her a helping hand. Pulling a long face, Old Lady Wei gave her an angry stare. Hong smiled. "Two will work more quickly than one."

Old Lady Wei uttered a greeting in her heart.

After they finished preparing the food, Old Lady Wei opened the door and pouted her lips, hinting that Hong should leave. Hong was patient enough to ignore her hint. She flashed her a disarming smile and took a feather duster to clean the furniture. Old Lady Wei was in a daze. She had to close the door after a moment. When she tidied up the room, Hong found

Xingguo's dirty underpants that needed to be washed. She took them to the sink and started washing them under the tap. Old Lady Wei seized the underpants. "Let him wash them by himself."

Hong snatched them back with a smile. "Men don't know how to wash clothes. Anyway, he will come back quite late. Don't burden him with housework."

She quickly finished washing Xingguo's underpants. Old Lady Wei could not help laughing. It seemed as if she was only Xingguo's stepmother whereas Hong was his own mother.

Xingguo came back home at night. When he saw that Hong was still there, he was wild with joy. He dared not ask too much. He glanced at his mother and was relieved when he found that she was not in a bad mood. Hong prepared dinner and it tasted the same as before. Still the three sat down together for the meal. Hong did not dare eat together with them and hesitated a moment. Only after Old Lady Wei told her to eat with them did she sit down at the table. Afterwards she volunteered to wash the dishes. She was more attentive than ever.

While she was doing the dishes, Xingguo drew up close next to her. "Did you make it up?"

Hong flashed him a faint smile without answering his question.

"Mom seems to be in a good mood," Xingguo continued.

Hong smiled again. A moment later Old Lady Wei moved toward her and patted her on the shoulder. "Let's take a walk. We need to have a talk."

Hong cast a glance at Xingguo, hoping he would stop them. To her dismay, the blockhead was delighted. "It's good to take a walk. The air is fresh outside."

With a wry smile, Hong put on her jacket and went out with Old Lady Wei.

They went down the stairs. Several neighbors greeted them. "Are you taking a walk?"

Old Lady Wei smiled lightly and nodded her head. Hong smiled, too. She was more confident because Old Lady Wei did not tell the neighbors about her betrayal. They strolled along slowly. The street lamplights elongated and shortened their shadows like a rubber band. The icy wind, though moderate, was biting. Their exposed faces and hands became reddened and numb with cold.

"I'll go back home alone," Old Lady Wei said.

"Don't follow me and don't go too far. We're both adults and we should have a sense of propriety."

Old Lady Wei turned back in the direction of her house without looking at her. Hong forced a smile and followed closely.

"It's no use following me. I meant what I said," Old Lady Wei continued. "You should know how to behave properly. Don't make us both lose face."

Hong halted her steps with hesitation and soon she was a distance from Old Lady Wei. She gritted her teeth and quickened her steps. She walked behind Old Lady Wei again. Old Lady Wei feigned obliviousness. When they reached the garden at a street intersection, Hong stopped abruptly. "Mom, I should be punished for my wrongdoing. As a self-imposed punishment, I'll sit here thinking about my betrayal. If you don't forgive me, I'll sit here all my life." With these words she sat bolt upright on the bench, hands folded in front of her.

This stunned Old Lady Wei. "Don't behave like this. I don't give in to threats."

Hong shook her head. "This is no threat. Mom, I really want to think a bit. If I had the intention of threatening you, I would take a stool and sit at the entrance of the lane."

Old Lady Wei gave a disgusted snort. "Do as you please."

She turned and walked away. When she got home, Xingguo asked her why Hong was not with her. As she was feeling sullen, she took the opportunity to vent her frustration on her son. "Other people bring up their children to provide for them in their old age. As for me, I bring you up to annoy me. I really gave birth to an utter blockhead. I think you must have been lacking some vital brain cells when you were born. How can you keep thinking about a woman like that? I reared you in vain. You're driving me mad!"

Old Lady Wei beat her bosom and stamped her foot in agony.

Xingguo left in a huff. Old Lady Wei went to the bathroom and washed her face. She sat down. One should keep calm, especially when things turn frustrating. This is the useful lesson she has drawn from her decades of life. If she is unable to hold back her anger, everything will be plunged into chaos.

Raindrops pelted down outside the window a moment later. The soaking rain has come at last.

Old Lady Wei guessed that Hong was putting

on a show outside. She would come back after a few more minutes and have a nice sleep. It was simply psychological warfare. The one who gives in first loses.

Old Lady Wei recalled a particular night that rained heavily. Holding five-year-old Xingguo in her arms, she went to Wuhu in Anhui Province. She went directly to the factory director's home immediately after she stepped off the ship. Her husband had worked on the ship all his life and was killed by a violent typhoon. The factory director alone decided the pension for the family of the deceased. The director offered a trifling sum, which Old Lady Wei refused to accept in any way. Though human life can't be measured by money, what else can remedy the pain of losing a loved one?

Old Lady Wei tried to persuade the director by citing the above reason again and again. Familiar with her reasoning, the director turned a deaf ear to her request. Old Lady Wei was so desperate that she, with her son in her arms, knelt down in front of the director's house. The rain was pouring down persistently. She helped her son into a raincoat. She herself knelt the whole night in the rain. The director did not care a bit. But his wife could not bear to see any more of it. "You may as well give her a generous pension. It's not easy for a widow with a little child. Their kneeling in the rain is unacceptable."

"If I give in this time, all the others will follow her example in the future. How can I run this factory then?"

Later, a policeman came and brought Old Lady Wei away. She did not expect to change the director's mind with her kneeling in the rain. She was well prepared for a lengthy battle. She did not expect to knock her opponent down with one stroke. The rub was to forestall one's opponent by a show of one's prowess. She would not let the director take a woman like her lightly. Old Lady Wei had warned her relatives before she came here. "It will take at least one week. If anything goes wrong, I may stay there for a couple of months."

Her father-in-law was a reasonable man. "Don't worry about us. Go and get it done."

However, her mother-in-law could not bear the loss of her son and seemed a little muddle-headed. She blamed Old Lady Wei. "You're a real money whore. What's the use of money when one is dead?"

Old Lady Wei did not mind others criticizing

her behind her back for "taking a dead man's money." Since everyone has a mouth, they have the freedom to use it to criticize. The mouth is the most annoying organ in the world. It is used to curse and it is used to eat. One can curse to one's great satisfaction and one can eat to one's heart's content. Old Lady Wei wanted to curse, too. She wanted to curse the typhoon, which was a once in a century phenomenon. She wanted to curse the factory director who had a heart of stone. But she knew very well that she was not in a position to curse. With her husband's death, all the mouths of her family, old and young, needed to be fed.

Old Lady Wei knelt there for several days. The police became gradually fed up. They could not hit a woman or a child. They failed to persuade her through reasoning. Finally, they helped Old Lady Wei in persuading the factory director. "Please make a compromise. No need to dispute with a widow."

The factory director did not give in because he must stick to his principle. His wife offered drinking water to Old Lady Wei several times and even gave Xingguo two pieces of candy. She herself had two sons. Her younger son was almost as old as Xingguo. She tried several times to persuade Old Lady Wei, but finally gave up. She brought out the cushion on which they knelt down to worship their ancestors and put it under Old Lady Wei's knees. "The ground is hard. Be careful to avoid hurting your knee joints."

She also explained for her husband, saying a big factory must be run according to strict rules. "Please allow for his difficulty," she said to Old Lady Wei. "He has no other choice. It's not his intention to irritate you."

"If I allow for his difficulty, who will allow for my difficulty?" Old Lady Wei said. "I don't want to make it difficult for him on purpose. I have no other choice either."

The two women talked back and forth as if practicing a tongue twister. Old Lady Wei and the director's wife, though staying respectively inside and outside the house, chatted with each other like sisters. Later, the director's wife even brought out a stool to keep her company. She helped Old Lady Wei hold her son while chatting and went back to her house only late at night. Old Lady Wei felt grateful to her for her kindness from the bottom of her heart. With the cushion underneath, she became more comfortable. Otherwise, her knees would have been badly bruised.

In retrospect, Old Lady Wei could not help but to heave a deep sigh. Decades have passed in the twinkling of an eye. Now the time has come for somebody else to threaten her. She wanted to go to the garden to see what had happened to Hong. After some initial hesitation, she restrained herself. She can't play into the hands of the little woman. Hong deliberately wanted to make it difficult for her to fall asleep. Old Lady Wei poured some warm water to the basin and sat down to wash her feet. Xingguo was whittling at a piece of bamboo nearby. The crooked bamboo chip showed that he was in no mood for his work.

Old Lady Wei was well aware that her son had been going in and out of trances these days. "She lives with her friend," Old Lady Wei said. "That girl who works as a maid in the next lane."

Xingguo remained silent. Old Lady Wei sighed. "If you find it hard to part with her, go and visit her as you please." With these words, she went to her bedroom. Lying in bed, she heard him watch television outside. He did not move at all. She was surprised that he could restrain himself like that. After a long while the sound of the television was still audible. Old Lady Wei became so impatient that she got up and walked out of her bedroom. She saw the television was still on, but there was nobody in the room. Old Lady Wei was both shocked and amused. She did not expect her son to do such a thing. She turned off the television and went back to bed.

The rain continued for the whole night. Xingguo avoided looking his mother straight in the eyes at breakfast the next day.

"Well, did you see her?" Old Lady Wei asked.

Xingguo flushed. "No."

Old Lady Wei knew he was not lying, but her heart skipped a beat. She was afraid that the little woman really sat in the garden for the whole night. If Hong became ill because she got wet in the rain that would be her fault. "She probably gave up and went back to Shangrao."

On her way to the market, Old Lady Wei deliberately made a detour to the garden at the street intersection. From a distance, she saw Hong sitting still on the bench like an old monk sitting in meditation. She hurried away for fear of being seen. She was worried. Hong is doing it for real!

In fact, Hong did not pass the whole night in the garden. As soon as Old Lady Wei left, she went back to Du Qin's house. She guessed that Old Lady Wei would come again to check. As was expected, Xingguo came to Du Qin's house. Du Qin stopped him at the door. "I'm not her mother. Why do you ask me for where she is?"

Hong hid herself in the inner room. When she heard Xingguo trying clumsily to explain, she wondered if he had really missed her after all. When Xingguo walked away, Hong made the bed and went to sleep. She planned to store up her energy for a lengthy battle. Du Qin reminded her that Old Lady Wei might go to the garden. Hong was smug. "She won't tonight. But she may go there tomorrow night."

"Are you sure?" Du Qin asked.

A trace of a smile played across her lips.

After she came back home from the market, Old Lady Wei was on pins and needles. She thought she had courted trouble this time. Not like the factory director in those days who could call the police, she had no right to report to the police. She still kept alive the hope that the little woman was engaged in tricks. When her son fell into a deep sleep that night, Old Lady Wei went to the garden quietly.

By the light of the street lamp, she saw Hong

sitting still on the bench. With half closed eyes and in a relaxed manner, she looked like a Buddha.

Old Lady Wei sucked in a deep breath.

The people in the lane knew their skirmish. The clever ones figured out the situation clearly at a glance. And then there were the seemingly clueless ones Old Lady Wei thought were pulling her leg. "Your daughter-in-law Hong is leading a very comfortable life, basking in the sun in the garden."

She decided to lay bare the truth. "She's no longer my daughter-in-law. She can do whatever she likes. It's none of my business."

Auntie Zhang did not expect things to get out of control like this. "It's a shame that smart people do foolish things."

"Our family is a temple that is too small to hold a huge Buddha like her," Old Lady Wei said.

"But it's also your fault," Auntie Zhang countered. "If you had made a prompt decision, things would not be like this."

Old Lady Wei did not buy into her argument, because Auntie Zhang was not the one hunting for a daughter-in-law. That's why had the luxury of making derisive comments from the sidelines.

"What shall we do?" Auntie Zhang asked. "It will be scandalous for such a Buddha to bask in the sun in the garden every day."

"Let her bask in the sun as much as she wishes."

She felt nervous even though she refused to admit her own role in this unfortunate matter. Fortunately, Hong only sat in the garden and did not disturb her life. The nearby garden was a few blocks away. Old Lady Wei was cross with Hong because the little woman treated her like a performing monkey and deceived her without even lifting her eyes. When she calmed down, she had to admit that the little woman did not go too far. If she had knelt down in front of her house, she would have made a bad mess of the matter.

In her opinion, Hong did not let her and her son lose too much face for the sole purpose of leaving some leeway for her. It's not like collecting debt at her doorstep. If she goes to extremes, she will get the worst of it. At the thought of this, Old Lady Wei felt somewhat relieved.

Behind his mother's back, Xingguo brought Hong something to eat. He bought some bread and cooked food for her.

"The more kind-hearted you are, the more guilty I will feel," Hong said. "You are a good man. Mom is a good woman. I feel extremely sorry for deceiving you both."

Xingguo did not care a bit. "It's just a little trick, not a betrayal. It doesn't matter. If you didn't really like me, you would not have done so."

Hong sighed. "You're too kind-hearted. That's why Mom is worried about you. Listen to me: you will suffer if you always think of others in a better light. I wonder which girl has the luck to marry you—"

"I don't want any girl except you."

Hong hung her head and was on the verge of tears. Xingguo stared at her and it made his heart ache to see her miserable. "Are you determined to sit here all your life?"

Hong shook her head. "I'll leave in a few days. Actually, I've straightened out my thinking. It is destiny for some people to be born under a lucky star and for others to have ill fortune. After I leave, you should live happily. I'll write to you often."

Xingguo choked with emotion. "Are you really going?"

"My home is not here. What can I do if I don't go?"

Xingguo stamped his foot. "I won't let you go."

Hong smiled. "Don't behave like a child. You're both kind-hearted and skillful. With your skills you can earn money and live an independent life. You don't need to depend on somebody else. Mom lives with great difficulty. You ought to treat her with more respect."

"I'm not going to get married for the rest of my life!" Xingguo announced to Old Lady Wei when he returned home.

Old Lady Wei was shocked. Xingguo went on. "If you insist on Hong leaving, I will stay single all my life. I rather die than marry someone else."

Old Lady Wei heaved a sigh of relief. "Leaving? Did she herself say that?"

Xingguo gave a snort of acknowledgment. "Yes, she said that. So what? Anyway, I won't let her go."

Old Lady Wei was amused. "Are you sure you won't let her go? Then you just ask her to stay. You two can buy a house and live there by yourselves. I won't give this house to you because I need it to provide for my old age."

Xingguo was willful. "Do whatever you like! I'll go to Jiangxi with her."

Old Lady Wei became even more amused. "Go to Jiangxi? That's good. Young people with high aspirations make their home everywhere, so long as you can get by."

"Of course we can get by." Xingguo recalled what Hong had said and threw out his chest. "I'm skilful. I know how to earn money. I can manage to live a decent life anywhere in the country. I don't need to depend on anybody else."

Old Lady Wei was taken aback. Her son's facial expression told her that he was not joking. She became agitated. "Now that your wings have become strong and you can fly by yourself, you don't need your mother anymore. Did Hong teach you that?"

Xingguo argued on Hong's behalf. "Hong is really a good woman. Even if you treated her like that, she still told me to treat you with more respect. She called you 'Mom' all the time as if you were her own mother."

Old Lady Wei could not take it anymore. "How did I treat her? She deceived me by pretending to be pregnant. Did I ever slap her face or force her to kneel on the washboard? I did not even spit out any harsh words. I sent her away in a good manner. What did you expect me to do? Do you want me to call her 'Mom' and kneel before her, begging her to come back?"

Old Lady Wei became more and more agitated and pounded the table with a heavy thump.

Xingguo conceded and kept his mouth shut.

Du Qin brought a lunch box to Hong every day. Hong felt ill at ease because something terrible had happened to Du Qin's family. The boss of the construction site failed to pay wages to hundreds of workers. Her husband volunteered to talk with the boss on behalf of his co-workers. He told his boss that since the Spring Festival was approaching, the workers were waiting for their payment before they went back home. It was wrong for the boss to act like that. He was beaten later by some thugs hired by the boss. He was so badly injured that he had to lie in bed for several days. Du Qin was an impetuous person and insisted that she would take them to court. The boss produced an eyewitness who testified that it was her husband who started the fight. The boss was sure that at most they would be penalized for exceeding the proper limits of self-defense. The boss gave them several thousand yuan for medical treatment as if they were beggars. Du Qin threw the banknotes to his face and told him that she would bring him to justice. She was discussing the case with a lawyer. Hong tried to persuaded her to give it up, reasoning that she would suffer herself if she threw eggs at a rock. Du Qin wouldn't hear it. She said she wanted to argue strongly on just grounds. Even if eggs would be broken to pieces, she would try her utmost to leave a mark on the rock.

Medical treatment cost money. Hiring a lawyer also cost money. She used up all her savings. She even sold at the second-hand shop the goods she had purchased for the Spring Festival, including the cigarettes and wine for her father, the wool sweater for her mother, and the stationery for her daughter. Even if she had sold everything, she still failed to collect enough money.

Du Qin told Hong she was prepared to sell her kidney to her employer. "The old man doesn't have any children and a good kidney, but he has money."

This frightened Hong. "Don't talk rubbish!"

Du Qin smiled. "Who talks rubbish? I've undergone a medical examination and am waiting for the day of operation."

Hong persuaded her to think twice. "You said yourself that kidneys are very important to everybody. Do you thing they're like hair that will grow back after you lose it?"

"I know kidneys are important, but getting justice is more important. I want that bastard to understand that I'm not a person to be trifled with."

She changed the subject and started to comfort Hong. "We have two kidneys and we can still live a healthy life with just one left."

Xingguo came to tell Hong that he wanted to elope with her. "It doesn't matter if my mother won't accept you. I'll go to Shangrao with you."

Hong was against his idea. "You're the apple of Mom's eye. How can you act like that? It will break her heart."

Xingguo was persistent with his idea. "I don't care. You're the only one I want. I only want you as my companion for the rest of my life. Without you, I would rather be a monk. I'll go with you to Shangrao and we'll spend the Spring Festival there."

That afternoon Old Lady Wei went to the garden to visit Hong. Hong was well prepared and was even equipped with facial tissues for wiping tears with. Before Old Lady Wei started to talk, tears of grief rolled down Hong's cheeks. "Mom!"

Old Lady Wei was almost disarmed by the intimate way Hong wailed, as if she was truly the little woman's mother. She looked around and saw some people pointing their fingers in their direction. Old Lady Wei heaved a deep sigh. She has become the most talked about old woman in the neighborhood.

She was about to talk when Hong uttered another "Mom." Hong could not fight back the flood of tears. There was a momentary hesitation before Old Lady Wei took out a handkerchief and handed it to her. Hong did not accept it and pointed to the tissues in her hand. "I have some."

Old Lady Wei was taken aback by surprise and squeezed her handkerchief into Hong's hand.

"Use my handkerchief. It's better for the environment." As soon as she said this, Old Lady Wei realized that she had lost this round.

"Thank you, Mom."

While wiping away her tears, Hong stole a glance at Old Lady Wei and saw her looking in her direction. The two women's eyes locked together and were glued to each other for a moment. Both of them appeared naked to each other and their masks were stripped off. Their hearts had a common beat and were linked together. After a brief hesitation, Hong felt a growing sense of guilt. Her coherent action of wiping her tears was interrupted and she no longer looked unaffected.

Old Lady Wei finally broke the long silence. "Are you determined to pester my son?"

It's your son who's pestering me, Hong thought. "Mom, I'm not pestering him. I like him."

Old Lady Wei cut her short with a wave of her hand. "Those flattering words of yours have turned my stomach."

Hong kept her mouth shut.

After a little while Old Lady Wei started to speak. "My son has been clamoring to go to Shangrao with you. Does that make you happy now?"

Then Old Lady Wei started to scold herself for her stupidity. She blamed herself for failing to hold back her emotions. As expected, Hong poured out her grievances. "Mom, that wasn't my intent. I tried my best to talk him out of it."

Old Lady Wei gave a derisive snort. "Yes, you are a decent person, the most decent person on earth."

Hong pouted her lips. Old Lady Wei stopped talking.

When Hong finally spoke, her voice was soft. "Mom, I don't want to go back to Shangrao. You should know that."

Old Lady Wei knew this was true.

"Mom, if you had not found out the facts, Xingguo and I would have gotten the marriage certificate," Hong said. "Even if I acted in my own interests, I would be nice to you. If you're happy, I'll be happy, and everybody will be happy. That's why I think, Mom, it's not always beneficial to know the truth."

Old Lady Wei thought about his and had to admit that Hong was right.

"Mom, can you just pretend that all of this never happened?" Hong pleaded.

Old Lady Wei pulled a straight face and said nothing, so Hong continued. "Look at those emperors in the TV series. They perpetrate evil deeds before they become emperors. But once they become emperors, they treat common people very well. Mom, I admit I made a mistake, a very serious one. But my sole purpose was to become your daughter-in-law.

Once I become your daughter-in-law, I'll be nice to you, and to Xingguo. I'll do all the household chores. I'll be the best daughter-in-law in Shanghai."

After saying this, Hong felt her chest puff up, her heart beat faster, and her eyes red-rimmed.

Old Lady Wei fixed her eyes on her. The last two remarks were really emotional and touching. She did not expect Hong to be so eloquent, even citing emperors to support her argument. Old Lady Wei deliberately gave a snort of contempt. "It's sunny today. Go on with your sitting."

She turned about and walked away.

Watching Old Lady Wei's receding figure turn and disappear, Hong stood up and pounded her back. Sitting still too long made her ache and numb all over. The warm but not glaring sun in the early afternoon touched her like a light and thin blanket. The sunshine gave off a faint smell of meat. Instead of being high and aloof, the sun seemed very cordial and intimate. Even the dust, which was drifting about with the wind, became very soft like a lover's hand brushing gently against her face.

Suddenly her mobile phone rang. It was a message from Xingguo. "It looks like rain tonight.

Let's go to the movies."

Hong could not help smiling. They would go to the movies only when it was raining. This was a secret between them. She took out a thermos mug, opened the lid and drank the tea prescribed by an experienced doctor of traditional Chinese medicine to increase her chances of conceiving. She had taken this medication for quite a while now. Hong counted the days on her fingers. Today would be an ideal day to conceive. It was an appropriate day to go to the movies. Du Qin had passed on to her some detailed and explicit tips on prescriptions for men and women, special drinks and food, and even lovemaking positions. It seems there were only a couple of days in each month just right for a woman to conceive. If you miss those days, you'll have to wait for a whole month. Usually people can wait, but Hong was out of time. People always say time means money. In Hong's mind, time means a check. If she doesn't cash it within a time limit, the check will become invalid. When you fail to get the amount of money written on the check, you'll be overwhelmed with anxiety. An invalid check will be like a life threatening charm to her.

The traditional Chinese medication was as bitter

as usual. But when she gulped it down, it would cover her heart with a ray of hope. Hong put back the thermos mug and let out a long breath. She sent a text message to Xingguo: "I've listened to the weather forecast. It will rain tonight for sure."

4

Not long after the Spring Festival, Du Qin's case was heard in court. She pushed the wheelchair with her husband in it to the courtroom. The black-hearted boss who stood in the defendant's box gave Du Qin a frantic look. No ruling was handed down at the first trial. Their lawyer concluded that the case was in their favor and they should pursue the lawsuit to the end.

"The lawyer urged you to pursue the lawsuit to the end in order to earn more money," Hong said to Du Qin. "Don't walk into that trap."

Du Qin was nonchalant. "I won't drop my lawsuit. It will please me to see the bastard suffer. I haven't widened my knowledge in the past few years since I came to Shanghai. My experience of going to court will be something I can boast about when I see my friends in Jiangxi."

Hong told her she was silly.

Du Qin smiled casually. "I can endure any hardship, but I won't allow anybody to take advantage of me. If somebody takes advantage of me, I won't let him off by any means. My husband said, even if we win the case, we're unable to stay in Shanghai any longer. As he works at a construction site, no other company in Shanghai will hire him as a construction worker anymore. We'll have to move to some other city to start over."

"Where are you prepared to go?" Hong asked.

"We haven't decided yet. Either Beijing or Guangzhou."

"Both are big cities."

Du Qin nodded. "Yes. We've stayed in Shanghai for such a long time. We've been spoiled here, We won't be used to living in a small city anymore."

Both of them burst into laughter.

The Resettlement Working Team decided to allocate to Old Lady Wei a two-bedroom apartment in Sanlin in the Pudong Area. Old Lady Wei wouldn't comply. "I've lived west of the Huangpu River for decades and I love the Puxi Area. I don't think I can get used to living east of the Huangpu River."

The Resettlement Working Team promised to grant her a financial compensation of fifty thousand yuan. Old Lady Wei just didn't accept that.

Their negotiation became deadlocked. Everyday Hong brought a small stool with her and sat in front of the office of the Resettlement Working Team. Old Lady Wei brought three meals to her. The original plan was that Old Lady Wei took part in a sit-down protest while Hong was responsible for bringing her the three meals. Hong thought it was more appropriate for her to sit in. "Since I'm pregnant, who would dare touch me? Anybody who touches me will get himself into trouble."

Old Lady Wei thought it was a clever idea. Compared with an old woman, a pregnant woman was in a more advantageous position.

Hong's swollen belly became more and more distinct. The leading member of the Neighborhood Committee visited Old Lady Wei several times, saying that it might do harm to a pregnant woman. Old Lady Wei refuted him. "We're in a modern age. A pregnant woman is not supposed to stay at home all day long. Fresh air and warm sunshine will be beneficial to her health. What's more, constant exposure to sunlight will enrich her calcium. This will save money in buying calcium tablets. It really serves two purposes at the same time."

The leading member of the Neighborhood Committee said it was a tough job for an old lady like her to send three meals every day. Old Lady Wei said she did not think so. "It's important for old people to get more exercise. If an old woman is too lazy to do any exercise, she will have stiff joints and fragile bones. Though I'm an old woman, I'm still tough and strong. Even seven or eight trips back and forth a day won't tire me out. Anyway, thank you for showing concern for me."

The compensation amount increased to one hundred thousand yuan. Old Lady Wei did not even lift blink an eye. Though one hundred thousand yuan was not a small sum for daily expenses, it meant nothing when you buy a house. Even in an area like Sanlin, you can only buy a bathroom with this sum. Old Lady Wei's goal was an additional two-bedroom apartment. She would give in grudgingly if she could achieve this goal.

Xingguo persuaded his mother to make a

concession because he thought it was getting troublesome. Hong stood firmly behind Old Lady Wei. "Mom, I'm at your command."

In Old Lady Wei's mind, her son was a good-for-nothing. House property is the best thing in the world. Savings in the bank may depreciate, but house property won't. House prices are going up every day with incredible speed. Every square meter you take possession of is worth your yearly salary. If you are reluctant to scramble for wealth, what's the point of living on earth? She'd rather die than live like that.

It was getting hotter and hotter. Hong chose to sit in the shade of a big tree. She was painting the carriage made from bamboo chips. It was her job to polish the semi-finished products made by Xingguo. The assembly line method saved Xingguo a lot of time. He could focus on making the initial products. As he received more and more online orders, Xinguo made use of every bit of his free time in the factory. He was caught twice moonlighting by his supervisor and was given a disciplinary warning. Xingguo was quite frightened.

"What's there to be afraid of?" Hong said. "If worst comes to the worst, you can quit. You can ask your supervisor about his monthly salary. Our income is more than five times as much as his."

Her inspiring remarks filled Xingguo with pride and enthusiasm. "I have good skills. I'm afraid of nothing."

"According to Marx, technology is the primary productive force."

"You know Marx's teaching?"

Hong cast a scornful look at him. "Do you think I'm like you who know nothing except going to the movies?"

Xingguo sniggered and went forward to embrace her. "It looks like rain tonight..."

Hong uttered a sound of disapproval. "Can't you see I'm with child? You won't get what you want even if it's hailing."

Hong's seating position looked very composed. Her way of sitting still produced a deterrent effect. When she brought her three meals, Old Lady Wei recalled the days several months ago when Hong sat in the garden at a street intersection.

"Ours was internal contradiction between people. Right now we are united against external forces," Hong said jokingly.

All right, so everyone knows the little woman is hard to deal with. Nobody will take her lightly, Old Lady Wei thought to herself.

That day Old Lady Wei helped Hong up in the garden. This scene was a demarcation line of historic significance. Before she was helped up, she was a little woman from Jiangxi. After she was helped up, she became a young wife living in Shanghai. Hong tried her best to remain composed, but she was so moved that her voice quivered. Old Lady Wei looked a bit moved, too.

For a brief instant she saw a hand swaying before her eyes—that of the factory director's wife, who helped her up in an affectionate manner. "Well, now, everything is settled."

In the end the factory director failed to bring her around and promised to double the pension for her. She had knelt in front of the director's house for three whole weeks. When she stood up, she had a sudden blackout. She felt weak in her legs and almost knelt down again. The director's wife propped her up firmly.

The kind-hearted woman seemed more overjoyed than she. "Well, well, everything is settled..." she said repeatedly.

Old Lady Wei could feel her sincere joy over her success. Old Lady Wei was a pretty young woman in her early 30s with a fair complexion and jet-black hair. The director's wife did not know that during the night when she went back to her parents' home, Old Lady Wei stood up, knocked at the door and got into the director's bed. Remarkable coincidences did happen in real life. The director's wife happened to go back to her parents' home that night. The director happened to get drunk that night. Old Lady Wei did hesitate for a minute, but she would not let this chance slip by. She put her son down on the floor. After putting her hair up, she sneaked into the director's bedroom like a snake. When she came out of the room a moment later, she was well aware that she had crossed the line. On this side, she was a shy young woman and on that side she was a staunch woman, who was tougher than a man. At the thought of the director's wife, Old Lady Wei felt guilty, but she had no regrets.

When Old Lady Wei touched Hong's course hands, a chill shot through her. Something is circulating in her heart and just for an instant it seems to pass through thousands of days and nights. It's the way days circulate—yesterday is today, today is tomorrow, and tomorrow is yesterday. Days go on like this. When Old Lady Wei put herself in Hong's place, one scene after another seemed to be reflected on the clear mirror. She had been leading a hard life. Full of sympathy for her hard life, Old Lady Wei reached for her hand and put it in her own hand.

"Try to live happily," Old Lady Wei said.

Members of the Neighborhood Committee visited them from time to time. Old Lady Wei would not give in. She and Hong were prepared for a lengthy battle. The apparent bulging of her belly added to the weight of Hong's sit-in. The members of the Resettlement Working Team were deeply troubled. Hong left early in the morning and came back late in the afternoon. She staged her sit-down protest as though she was going to work every day. She was full of confidence. Old Lady Wei was full of confidence, too. While engaging in lengthy battle, women always gained the upper hand.

In the end, Du Qin did not donate her kidney, because her husband forced her to yield by threatening to commit suicide. Though she had signed a letter of consent, Du Qin was compelled to annul the contract. Her husband was resolute. "You came to

Shanghai with two healthy kidneys. You ought to leave Shanghai with your two kidneys intact. Not a single one should be missing."

Du Qin smiled. "You don't make any sense. Our opinions should change according to the actual situation."

"Think of our daughter Crescent Moon."

What he said touched Du Qin. Crescent Moon is still a seven-year-old child. How can a mother with only one kidney take good care of her?

They sold their house in their hometown and borrowed from everybody.

"If I had known then, I would have accepted those several thousand yuan," Du Qin said to Hong.

"You can't feed yourself on face-saving."

"What's the use of putting on a good show? After one is starved to death, he won't have any chance to show anything."

She said jokingly that she would like to find that bastard and get the money back. Hong laughed at her, telling her friend that she was a few cards short of a full deck.

Du Qin showed the photo of her daughter to Hong. "That's my Crescent Moon. Isn't she pretty?"

Hong looked carefully at the photo. "She looks more like you."

"Of course. If she takes after her father, it will be terrible. With a big mouth and an upturned nose, she won't be able to get married."

On the day when Du Qin and her husband left Shanghai, Hong saw them off at the railway station.

"Is it a he or a she?" Du Qin asked, glancing at Hong's bulging belly.

"The doctor turned down my request. But my mother-in-law said, since my pointed belly looks like a stone of a date, it must be a he."

"So you have a good fortune."

Hong smiled. "Shanghai people don't care whether I'll give birth to a baby boy or a baby girl."

On the bus going home, Hong sat in a window seat. She laughed in private. It was sheer nonsense that a pointed belly means one will have a boy. When she gave birth to her first child, her belly was pointed, but her first child was a girl. The day of her delivery was the 15th of the lunar month. The moon was as round as a ball. That's why she gave her baby girl the pet name "Full Moon." Her daughter is 10 years old now. As Du Qin's daughter was called Crescent

Moon, it was a happy coincidence that her daughter was named Full Moon.

The red packet she had given to the matchmaker served to open a door for her and silence the matchmaker at the same time. Other women with their own children would never entertain such an idea. But Hong didn't recoil with fear. People make new paths all the time. So long as she was determined, she could walk any path beset with difficulties. At that time, she was ready to risk everything. She was still scared whenever she thinks of what has happened.

Her plan wasn't realistic now. Hong wanted to bring Full Moon to Shanghai in a few years. Her child must be with her. A mother and her daughter must live together. Then Full Moon will become Shanghai's Full Moon. It may be difficult to implement this plan. But Hong doesn't worry at all. It's still too early to worry about that. There's plenty of time. Nobody can foretell his or her future. Hong is confident.

A crystal clear warm and moist breeze wafted in through the window. The swaying branches full of leaves looked like drunken men. Bathed in brilliant sunshine, the road was full of golden imprints. It was such a beautiful scene.

A Riot of Brilliant Purple and
Tender Crimson

1

"What a riot of brilliant purple and tender
  crimson
Among the ruined wells and crumbling walls
What an enchanting sight on this fine morning."

Her father's singing of the Kunqu opera had woken
up Xiang Yijun before dawn. She got out of bed
and opened the door quietly. Her father Xiang Hai
had shut tightly all the doors and windows of the
living room and drawn the curtains. He waved the
long sleeves of his pleated costume gracefully. His
waist was still soft and his posture was elegant. He
turned his head, curled his lips, lifted his eyes, and
raised his orchid-shaped fingers—all these theatrical
movements transformed him into Du Liniang, the
female lead in the play *The Peony Pavilion*.

Xiang Hai lowered his voice and swallowed some
high-pitched notes. Yijun knew her father was afraid

of disturbing their neighbors, which is why he wasn't singing to his heart's content. But it didn't matter. The living room was not a stage and her father's performance was simply for his own amusement, not for the applause of an audience. Xiang Hai enjoyed a brief spell of intoxication, just like fish swimming back to the sea and birds flying back to the forest. That kind of satisfaction was beyond words and etched deeply into his mind. At that moment, he felt as though he lived in another world. He need only close his eyes to enjoy the enchanting sight around him.

Yijun closed the door and went back to bed. She did not want to disturb her father, so she feigned sleep. A while later Xiang Hai knocked on the door and called out, "Yijun, it's time to get up."

"OK!" She called back and got up, put on her clothes, and went to the bathroom. After brushing her teeth and washing her face, she went to the living room. Breakfast was on the table—porridge, salted tender leaves of Chinese toon, crab meat gruel, two pieces of toast with a poached egg, and a glass of milk. Xiang Hai was fastidious about food and breakfast was no exception. His grandfather—Yijun's great grandfather—was a famous *jinghu* performer in

Shanghai. Though he did not come from a wealthy and influential family, he enjoyed all the comforts of luxury. Influenced by his grandfather, Xiang Hai learned Beijing opera and Kunqu opera. With a good voice and excellent stage appearance, he was the pillar of the Beijing opera troupe specializing in performing Mei Lanfang-style female roles. As his voice began to go, he changed to performing Kunqu opera. But as time went on, he stopped performing and stayed at home.

Yijun quietly studied her father while she ate her breakfast. Xiang Hai was clean shaven and there was a greenish lime patch on his chin. It was the established rules for the male performers of female roles to be clean shavened with no sign of a beard or moustache. His Braun shaver was imported and his shaving cream and aftershave were top-grade. He got into the habit of examining himself in the mirror after each shave. Whenever he saw beard stubble, he would feel uncomfortable, as if he had been infested with lice. After shaving himself, he always lifted his orchid-shaped fingers to stroke his chin and cast a look in the mirror. He ended this procedure with a freeze-frame posture.

Yijun glanced at the clock on the wall—it was

seven o'clock. She was pressed for time to get to work, but she still ate her meal slowly. Her father had always told her: "Even if you're faced with an urgent matter, you must take it easy so as not to disrupt your good posture. It's especially so for girls." So Yijun swallowed the last bite of toast in a composed manner before she stood up and took her bag. "Dad, I'm going to work."

Xiang Hai nodded his head slightly and raised his hand to wave to her gracefully.

"Go," he said in his Beijing opera voice. "Take care."

Yijun worked at Customs at the airport.

When she graduated from high school, she intended to apply to the Traditional Chinese Opera Institute because she was interested in it, and because it would please her father. Like him, Yijun had an oval face. Though her features were regular and symmetrical, she was not considered as beautiful. Her father said these kinds of facial features are especially suited for playing a female role in a traditional opera. When the plain looking features are made up, the performer's facial expression will become lively. The time before she filled out the application form, she often practiced waving long white sleeves and singing several lines of Beijing opera in the presence of her father. She thought he had firmly supported her intentions. She did not know he changed his mind after her uncle's visit.

Her uncle loved her dearly and after her mother died, he came to visit Yijun frequently. As a businessman, he was experienced and knowledgeable. "Your dad behaves like an alien. Be sure not to follow his example." Yijun could only smile as a response.

Xiang Hai did not get along with his brother-in-law. When they meet, Xiang Hai would smile politely, but talked little. However, he treated him with courtesy. He always entertained him with tea and refreshments. When his brother-in-law left, he always walked him downstairs to the door and waved to his receding figure.

"Take care, my daughter's uncle." Xiang Hai uttered these soft farewells out of politeness.

"Tell your dad not to speak like this. It gives me goose bumps all over," her uncle pleaded with Yijun. Still, she could only smile as a response.

Yijun knew her father best. The tacit understanding between them was inherent. It was not something forced or feinted by them. Before she learned to speak, she had listened to her father sing the opera. In the beginning, she thought her father's singing was fun. But gradually, she became more involved in it. In the end, she enjoyed it so much that she wished she could travel back to that time a thousand years ago and stay there. Everything about the characters of the opera was real to her; their breathtaking beauty, their colorful costumes, their vivid eye movements and changing facial expressions.

Yijun is a fan of popular songs. But popular songs are no match for the Beijing and Kunqu operas. The former is like a preserved plum in her mouth while the latter is like a cup of pure and strong tea. As soon as she catches its lingering and aromatic smell, she becomes slightly intoxicated. Yijun tends to forget pop songs after she listens to them, but the melody of the opera evokes strong repercussions in her heart. When the performer stops singing, she is still absorbed like a fool.

When she was a child, Yijun was sent to buy soy sauce from the grocery. On the way, she used to sing the lines from the Beijing opera *Drunken Imperial Concubine.*

"A moon appears behind the island in the sea.
I see the moon rising in the east.
The bright moon gradually leaves the island—"

She walked with quick short steps, fixed her eyes on nothing but concrete, and kept muttering the lines. She was so absorbed that people walking past jokingly called her a stupid girl. They were certain that she would behave just like her stupid father when she grew up.

While Yijun sang the Beijiing opera, Xiang Hai, with a cigarette between his fingers, beat time on the table with his hand. Yijun had a brighter voice and more graceful posture than her father. When an actor played a female role, his stage appearance was a little bit awkward.

"The four famous female role performers were all men," Xiang Hai explained. "Men understand better the beauty of a woman than women do." He then added, "today's famous performers can't hold a candle to the four all time greats. They lack something. Movie and TV stars are on the rise in this changing world. But outstanding opera performers are nowhere to be found."

Yijun was a talented Beijing opera performer. Instructed by her father, she had won the municipal Beijing opera amateur performers' contest at the children's level without any professional training. When she went onto the stage to be awarded the prize, the hostess of the ceremony asked her what she wanted to be when she grew up. Without thinking, she answered, "A famous actress." Though she usually spoke with a Shanghai accented Mandarin, she said "a famous actress" in the standard Beijing dialect, which set the whole theatre rocking with laughter.

One month before the university entrance examination Yijun showed her completed application form to her father. Her uncle came to visit them that day. When he saw the completed form, he firmly objected to her idea. "What a fool you are! What substantial benefit can you gain from performing the traditional Chinese opera? Can you name any performers who have made impressive achievements? Your dad was a performer and you want to be one. You can judge the advantages of being a performer from the example of your dad."

Her uncle attempted to talk her out of the idea for her own good. He tried so hard that he made indiscreet remarks about her father. Xiang Hai remained silent. He took the cup of tea from the table, lifted the lid and blew away the tea scum. But he put down the cup without taking a single sip.

"Even if you dream of flying in the sky all day long, you have to land on the ground at the critical juncture. You should see the outside world—a much changed world. Do you think the real world is the imagined one in the operas?" Her uncle said before he left.

That night Xiang Hai had trouble falling asleep. The light of his bedroom was on all night. Though the door of his room was shut, the smell of his cigarettes wafted out of the room. Yijun was also awake all night. Lying in her bed, she imagined a scene in her head—her father standing inside the door wanting to move his foot forward, but could not stride across the room. It was noisy outside the door and very quiet inside. He covered his ears with his beautiful orchid-shaped fingers.

The next day, her father asked Yijun to change

her selected academic discipline into business management in her application form. To her surprise, Yijun saw for the first time that her father had forgotten to shave. His thick beard and moustache extended to his cheeks. Her father heaved a deep sigh that vibrated in the air for a long time and then stopped abruptly. She could almost hear the thick phlegm in his throat. Shaking his head, her father turned round and walked into his bedroom

Clad in her Customs uniform, Yijun stood in front of her father. Xiang Hai fastened his eyes on her epaulettes for a while and then said, "A girl looks like a soldier when wearing this uniform."

Yijun responded, "A female martial role."

Xiang Hai cracked a smile, but kept silent.

As time passed, Yijun still indulged in her love of performing the Beijing opera. She spent half an hour every day practicing under her father's tutelage. During this half hour, Yijun, wearing her hair in a bun and theatrical makeup, immersed herself in waving the long white sleeves of her costume in a splendid and dazzling way, imagining the stage surrounded by small bridges across a flowing stream, pavilions, and

They don't seem to understand you. What matters is that you should understand yourself and what kind of person you are and what kind of people they are!"

Yijun listened to her father and became lost in her thoughts. She knew his remark implied a lot, but she could not grasp its meaning. She felt a constriction of the chest and the stuff that had filled it was overflowing. She had an irritated sensation in the nose, but this time her sentiment was different from that of being wronged. She herself could not tell what it was.

2

Yijun attended a year-end get together with her former classmates. They had not seen each other for a long time since graduation. They were exceptionally warm toward each other at the reunion. While having their barbecue, they drank red wine to their hearts' content. Even Yijun, who had never drank before, was in such high spirits that she consumed two glasses of red wine. Under the influence of the wine, she became talkative.

A young attendee wearing a leather jacket attracted her attention at the reunion. Since he was not her former classmate, she did not know how he had got in. He was probably a friend of her classmate. He did not drink or eat. He was busy selling insurance policies. He was distributing his business cards to everybody. Yijun got one, too. When she saw his name, she burst into laughter and said, "Mao An? How could your parents give you such a name?"

An was taken aback and asked her, "What is wrong with my name?"

Yijun belched. "It does sound a little bit weird—Mao An, Mao An, it sounds like a domestic help of the Mao family. In the old days, the rich and influential families liked to call their domestic help 'An.' If the master's surname is Zhang, his domestic help will be called Zhang An. If the master's surname is Wang, his domestic help will be called Wang An. Do you know the story about the famous painter Tang Bohu in the Ming Dynasty? In order to court the pretty girl Qiu Xiang, Tang Bohu volunteered to work as a domestic help in the Hua family and was renamed Hua An."

An stared at her. With her face glowing, Yijun said excitedly, "I'm not lying to you. You can check

with the book to see whether I'm telling the truth—"
But she broke into a fit of giggles before she could
finished her words.

An let out a little chuckle. "What's your name?"

"Xiang, yi, jun."

"What a beautiful name! Just like the name of
the leading female character in the scripts written
by the famous Taiwan writer Qiong Yao," An said.
"By the way, do you want to buy an insurance
policy? Since you're a young girl, I recommend a
new insurance policy from our company designed
especially for ladies. I guarantee you that it's a good
buy."

Yijun shook her head. "I don't buy any insurance
policies. Do you know why? My good friend's
brother works at an insurance company. He receives a
handsome salary and substantial benefits. His annual
bonus amounts to eighty or a hundred thousand
yuan. Every year he enjoys a free trip to Europe.
The insurance company makes such a fortune at the
sacrifice of the insurance policy holders. You persuade
us to buy insurance policies for the sole purpose of
swindling our money. And that's why I never buy an
insurance policy."

An was at a loss for words, but he heard an old classmate of Yijun's nearby say, "Yijun, sing us a piece of aria. We haven't heard your singing for a long time. We all miss your performance."

With a smile, Yijun stood up and walked to the center of the room. She bent her knees and bobbed a curtsy to all those present. She cleared her throat and sang an aria from the Beijing opera *Su San Being Sent Away under Escort*. As this was a very popular piece, her relaxed singing was pleasant and enjoyable to her former classmates. When it was over, they shouted in unison, "Encore!"

Yijun readily obliged and sang another popular piece entitled "I Have Countless Uncles."

After she had finished singing, Yijun went back to her seat. An came over to her. "How come you can sing so well? Did you receive any special training?"

Before she can open her mouth to respond, a nearby classmate of answered for her, "Yijun's father was part of the Beijing opera troupe."

"Did you know a girl name Yu Feifei in the troupe?" An quickly asked.

Yijun thought for a while. "No. My dad may know her. I'll ask him when I go back home."

"No, don't bother! I was just wondering that's all."

As soon as she got home that night, Yijun went to bed. She did not wake up until noon the next day with a terrible headache. When she recalled what had happened the night before, she vaguely realized that she had behaved foolishly under the influence of alcohol. She remembered An, enthusiastic young man who kept on nagging and even over exaggerated her condition. At the thought of this, Yijun became very upset. Her father was strongly against a girl drinking in public. She got up and took a bath. She brushed her teeth thoroughly in order to get rid of the alcoholic smell. To rule out the slightest risk, she brushed her teeth again. When she walked into the living room, her father was sitting on the sofa reading a newspaper.

"Dad!" Yijun greeted him before sitting down to her breakfast. But all of a sudden, she remembered something. "Do you know a girl name Yu Feifei who works at the Beijing opera troupe?"

Xiang Hai shook his head. "I don't know most of the newcomers."

After breakfast Yijun accompanied her father to

the market. When she opened the door, their neighbor Luo Manjuan came out from the next door. She had on a cream-colored wool skirt and was wearing her hair in a ponytail. Yijun called her "Auntie Luo."

Luo Manjuan's husband worked as a clown at the Beijing opera troupe before he died of liver cancer two years ago. He left behind his wife and son, who was in junior high school. In her early 40s, Luo Manjuan's pretty eyes and brows were clouded with her private grief. When she caught sight of Xiang Hai, she gave a slight nod of acknowledgement. "Master Xiang." Then she went down the staircase.

When she arrived downstairs, she opened the burglar proof door. She was about to close the door when she saw Xiang Hai and his daughter come downstairs. She held the door open for them.

"Thank you!" Xiang Hai said, hurrying up a bit. He smelled a faint scent coming from her. He was so stirred that he cast his eyes at her. Their eyes locked on each other before they both turned away.

"Bye bye," Luo Manjuan said softly.

Xiang Hai intended to say something more, but thought it might be cumbersome to comfort her. He fastened his eyes on her receding figure. Glowing in the morning sunlight, her golden figure appeared to be enveloped by the fog and became indistinct.

Xiang Hai usually didn't watch TV at home. When he turned it on, he was only interested in two channels—the traditional opera channel and the art channel. His favorite traditional opera channel broadcast a whole play of the Beijing opera during the day and some arias in the evening. After eight o'clock the channel became the program "Shopping on TV," promoting the sale of a great variety of goods. The art channel focused on broadcasting Shanghai-dialect farce, acrobatic performances, and several TV series. He was fed up with those dull jokes and noisy programs. The more he watched, the more dissatisfied he became. How could an art channel deliver such meaningless garbage?

Every evening on the art channel there was a fixed program of a Shanghai-dialect comedy called *Unconfirmed Stories about Old Uncle.* Every episode was a story that happened in the residential quarters. Most of the performers were from the farce troupe. Only one actor was a Beijing opera performer who sang a couple of arias from time to time to create a convivial atmosphere. Xiang Hai knew this performer was called Bai Wenli. He and Bai Wenli learned the Beijing opera from the same master and Bai Wenli was junior to him. Now, Bai Wenli was the deputy head of the Beijing opera troupe. Xiang Hai felt Bai Wenli's singing was not as good as before. In recent years, Bai Wenli had been busy with his stage appearances. He performed skits, farces, and even reversed roles. As a result, he did not make any progress in his own profession. However, he had become a household name, even more famous than those performers who had been awarded the Plum Blossom Prize.

A banging noise came from upstairs. The couple living on the fifth floor both worked at the Beijing opera troupe. Unfortunately, these two decent and law-abiding people had an unworthy son. Their son became a compulsive gambler when he was young. After he gambled away his own money, he took his parents' money to gamble with. His bad habit threw the whole family into chaos.

A glass object fell heavily on the floor. It was followed by a heated quarrel. After a long while the dispute was finally resolved. It became calm.

Xiang Hai shook his head. He turned on his

computer and went online to chat. Yijun taught him how to get online. If he idled away his time, it would become solidified. When he chatted on the Internet, time became liquefied and passed quickly.

Xiang Hai had a regular online friend called Liu Mengmei. Liu Mengmei is the name of the leading male character in the Kunqu opera *The Peony Pavilion*. When Xiang Hai went online for the first time six months ago, he picked up a cyber name: Du Liniang. He chatted online simply for fun. Not long after, Liu Mengmei appeared online.

"Are you female?" Liu Mengmei asked.

Xiang Hai replied: "I'm Du Liniang in my dreams. Why should you care whether I'm female or not? Since you're called 'Liu Mengmei,' are you male?"

"Just like you, I am Liu Mengmei in my dreams. Why should you care whether I'm male or not?"

With conversations like this, they became friends on the Internet. Xiang Hai was slow at typing and it took him a long time to finish a message. Liu Mengmei never pushed him and was a patient listener. Xiang Hai's words were more like lyrical prose than ordinary network chatting.

"Yesterday a leaf drifted by and fell down on my balcony. I picked it up and found it had turned slightly red. I knew we're already in the fall. That's the very meaning of the Chinese proverb 'the falling of one leaf heralds the coming of the fall.'"

In which Liu Mengmei said: "The fall wind is blowing. Have you ever smelled the wind? In fact, the smell of the wind in different seasons is entirely different. The spring wind gives off a smell of soil; the summer wind gives off a smell of moisture and fish; the fall wind gives off a smell of burned earth; the winter wind gives off a smell of cold cement."

"You've undertaken a thorough study. Next time I will smell the wind carefully. I guess you're a very careful person," Xiang Hai said. "Do you like to listen to traditional operas?"

"Yes, I do," Liu Mengmei replied. "I especially like the Beijing and Kunqu operas. Since you call yourself 'Du Liniang,' you must be a traditional opera lover. Am I right?"

After a momentary hesitation, Xiang Hai said, "In addition to listening, I performed traditional operas for decades."

They continued chatting online for the next

six months, meeting on the Internet every couple of days. Xiang Hai thought their encounter online was by fate. He called himself Du Liniang. It was a happy coincidence that somebody was called Liu Mengmei. It was said the social network was chaotic. He did not expect to meet a net pal who shared a common interest. It was truly a rare opportunity.

Today, Xiang Hai was frank with Liu Mengmei. "I'm in love with the woman next door." He felt his heart leapt and his face flushed. "Now you know I'm a man."

After a short pause Liu Mengmei asked, "Does the woman like to listen to traditional operas?"

"I don't know, but her ex-husband was a Beijing opera performer. Under his daily influence I don't think she dislikes traditional operas."

"In that case, go and tell her."

Xiang Hai stopped typing for a while. "I don't know what to say to her."

As soon as he typed this message, Xiang Hai went offline. With his heart beating rapidly, he stared blankly at the TV screen. He regretted having revealed his secret to his net pal. He had thought that it might be a relief for him to speak his mind. On the contrary, he was plunged into a state of indecision and agony.

Yijun got a phone call at her work.

"Hi, this is Mao An."

Yijun was in a daze. An instant later she came to herself. "Hi!" She felt a little uneasy about the fact that she had acted in an ill manner the other day. "It's you. What can I do for you?"

"I want to learn the Beijing opera from you."

"What?" Yijun did not believe her ears.

"I said I want to learn the Beijing opera from you." An raised his voice and repeated his request.

They agreed to meet at a café after work. Yijun stepped into the café and found An was already there. They both ordered coffee. An got straight to the point.

"I want to learn the Beijing opera from you. I'm not kidding. I'm very serious."

Yijun found this amusing. "I'm only a little better than an amateur, so I'm in no position to teach you. There are quite a few professional performers living in our residential compound. I can recommend someone to you."

An shook his head. "I don't need a professional actor for my teacher. I have no intention to be on the stage. I only want to master the basics."

Yijun cast a curious glance at him. "Why do you want to learn the Beijing opera?"

An lifted his cup and took a sip of coffee before smiling. "No special reason. You'll laugh at me if I tell you the truth. But you're already my master. It doesn't matter if the master laughs at her pupil. Do you still remember the Yu Feifei I mentioned to you the other day? You already know what I'm going to say next, right?" He stroked his head and cracked a grin. He was suddenly shy.

Yijun felt confused at first, but realized the truth in an instant. She laughed. "You're really an interesting guy."

"I'm not interesting at all. I'm serious, extremely serious," An said with emphasis. "I'm a person who will do a great job if he is motivated. I'll get fully prepared and I won't fight an unprepared battle. Only when you know both yourself and your enemy can you win every battle you fight. I'll try my best to defeat my enemy in one stroke." He became more and more excited.

Yijun couldn't help laughing louder. "You treat courting a girl like you're going to fight a battle."

She had intended to decline his request, but now she changed her mind. She wanted to participate in this game—this was something she had never experienced before. She was eager to try. Rolling her eyes, she asked, "Is Yu Feifei a beautiful girl?"

"Of course!"

When she got back home after work, Yijun saw a white Honda Accord parked in front of their compound. She recognized the car as Bai Wenli's. She went upstairs and opened the door. As expected, she saw Bai Wenli sitting on the sofa. Clad in a casual suit and holding a cup of tea in his hand, he talked happily with Xiang Hai.

"Uncle Bai," Yijun greeted him.

"So Yijun is back home," Bai Wenli said with a smile. "I haven't seen you for months. You've become more beautiful."

Bai Wenli set up a traditional opera school not too long ago, which attracted many students. He came to visit Xiang Hai today for the purpose of inviting him to be a teacher at his school.

Xiang Hai declined his invitation. "I haven't performed the traditional opera for a long time and I'm completely out of practice."

Bai Wenli flashed him a smile. "My senior co-learner, you can stall off other people with this excuse, but I won't buy it. To be frank, I trust nobody except you. If you accept my invitation, my school will be almost a success."

Xiang Hai shook his head. "My junior co-learner, I'm flattered by your praise. Now I'm an old and useless man. I don't know how to show them the ropes. If you invite me to be a teacher, the good reputation of your school will be damaged."

Bai Wenli smiled faintly. "My senior co-learner, you're too modest. You're a victim of your early retirement. If you keep on performing on the stage, nobody will outshine you. Would you please do me a favor? I hope you'll accept my offer for my sake and for the sake of those students as well. What's more, you'll make indelible contributions to the development of the quintessence of Chinese culture. Don't you think so?"

Xiang Hai sighed softly and kept silent.

Xiang Hai asked Bai Wenli to stay for supper. Bai

Wenli was glad to dine with them. He offered to help with the preparation of supper. Xiang Hai pushed him out of the kitchen. Bai Wenli walked to Yijun's room. He was surprised to see her reading a thick volume of *A Collection of Representative Plays of the Beijing Opera*.

"How come you're reading this book?" He asked in surprise.

"That's not my preference," Yijun said. "But as somebody wants to learn the Beijing opera from me, I have to prepare my lessons."

Bai Wenli smiled broadly. "It's a happy coincidence. I invited your dad to teach and somebody wants to learn under your instruction. Both of you become teachers."

Yijun shook her head and smiled. "I'm no teacher at all. I take up this job simply for fun. Besides, that student of mine does not have a pure motive. Do you know why he wants to learn the Beijing opera...?"

All of a sudden, she remembered the name that An had mentioned. "Uncle Bai, do you know Yu Feifei?"

Bai Wenli hesitated a little. "Yes, I do. She was assigned to work at our troupe last year. She specializes in acting the Chen-style female role. Do you know her?"

"No, I don't. But my pupil does."

Bai Wenli stayed for a while after supper and then stood up to take leave. Xiang Hai said he was going to walk him to the door and Bai Wenli declined. Xiang Hai told Yijun to walk him downstairs on his behalf. Yijun led the way and both of them walked downstairs in a slow pace until Bai Wenli halted abruptly. "You walk in the same manner as your mother."

Yijun stared at him blankly. "Really?"

"Yes." Bai Wenli fixed his eyes on her. "You two not only walk in the same way, but also look alike."

Yijun cracked a smile. "My uncle has the same opinion. But he said I'm not as pretty as my mom. My mom had an oval face and a straight nose. I have a flat nose and it looks like an onion."

Bai Wenli could not help laughing. "You're more serene than your mom. On the stage she was a *huadan* role while you're a *qingyi* role."

A *huadan* role is suited for lively and clever young girls while a *qingyi* role is suited for virtuous and elite ladies.

Xiang Hai turned on his computer and saw Liu Mengmei online.

"Have you had supper?" Liu Mengmei asked.

"I've just finished my meal. Today, my junior co-learner came to visit me."

"So your junior co-learner learned the Beijing opera together with you. Of you two, who is the better performer?" Liu Mengmei asked.

"It's hard to say. But so far as the present circumstances are concerned, he fares much better than I. We are two very different people. I'm only a performer whereas he's quite a character."

Xiang Hai stopped typing for a while and then continued. "I've never talked with anybody about this. I have no intention to play down his achievements. I only want to express my sentiment."

"I know what you mean."

Xiang Hai fastened his eyes on the five words on the screen and was at a loss how to answer. All sorts of feelings welled up in his heart and appropriate expressions escaped him. "Do you like the present world, Liu Mengmei?"

"Whether you like it or not, you can only live in this world. Do you have a time-and-space shuttle?"

Xiang Hai thought for a while. "I don't need a time-and-space shuttle. I simply draw the curtain, put on a stage costume, and close my eyes. Then another world appears in front of me." Then his face creased into a smile and laughed at himself for his stupidity. He shook his head.

"Have you talked with the woman next door?" Liu Mengmei asked suddenly.

Xiang Hai was surprised. "About what?"

"Bare your heart to her," Liu Mengmei said.

Xiang Hai hesitated and kept silent. After a long while he said, "I'm going to bed. Let's talk next time." He hurriedly went offline. He sat and stared blankly for a few minutes before he stood up. He walked to the balcony and raised his head to look at the stars in the sky. He turned his head to one side and glanced at a figure on the balcony next door. He saw with the aid of moonlight that it was Luo Manjuan. Both of them were dumbfounded when their eyes met.

"Oh, you haven't gone to bed yet, have you?" Xiang Hai asked after giving a dry cough.

"No." With a swing of her hand, Luo Manjuan hung the washed woolen sweater on a hanger.

"You air dry the sweater at night. Don't you

worry about it getting wet from dew drops?" Xiang Hai asked.

"The woolen sweater dries slowly. If I air dry it tomorrow, it won't get dry even after a whole day."

"Oh," Xiang Hai was at a loss for words. He raised his head again and held tightly on the rail. He feigned that he was looking at the stars, but he was actually searching for a topic for conversation. For fear that she might go back to her room after she finished hanging the sweater, he felt ill at ease. Nevertheless, he pretended and wore a broad smile, looked carefree and at ease.

"Master Xiang, I heard you singing this morning," Luo Manjuan said suddenly.

"Did I wake you up?"

"No, I was already awake. Even if I wasn't, it would be a delight to be waken up by such a melodious sound." She made this remark as she straightened out the wet sweater.

Xiang Hai was touched and had a desire to say something more. Just then Luo Manjuan turned around and walked to her room. "Good night!" She was a native of Suzhou. Her sweet and soft Suzhou dialect was a feast for the ears.

"Good night!" Watching her receding figure, Xiang Hai was restless and nostalgic, as if her words stirred up billows of emotion deep down in his heart. All this gave unsettled him and he lost his train of thought.

3

Yijun selected the nearby high school as the place for her lesson with An. On Saturdays and Sundays you could see students playing ball games on the playground. There was nobody in the classrooms. Yijun chose a classroom on the ground floor.

"I'll first talk about the origin of the Beijing opera," Yijun said in her first lecture. "The Beijing opera originated from the Anhui opera and the Hubei opera. During the reign of Emperor Qianlong in the Qing Dynasty, the Anhui opera troupe entered Beijing and cooperated with the performers of the Hubei opera. They absorbed the tunes and acting technique of the Kunqu opera and the Shaanxi opera and developed a new type of opera—the Beijing opera—"

"Master," An said. "Can you skip the theoretical knowledge and teach me how to sing and act?"

"Which aria would do you like to learn?"

"I have no idea. Any melodious aria will do. I hope it's not too difficult. You know I have no rudimentary knowledge about the Beijing opera."

"Then let's start with the aria *Su San Being Sent Away under Escort*."

"I know how to sing this piece!" An exclaimed excitedly. He volunteered to sing the whole aria. After he finished singing, he glanced at Yijun and smiled. "I know my singing is poor. Please don't look at me like that. I feel so self-conscious."

Yijun shook her head. "The problem is not if your singing is good or poor. You directed your breath in a wrong way. You should exert the deep breath that's controlled by the diaphragm. When you sing this way, you will produce a deep and sonorous voice. At present, your voice is light and thin, just like singing pop songs."

"Where's the diaphragm?" An asked. "How can I exert the deep breath controlled by the diaphragm?"

"The diaphragm is under the belly. Try to take a deep breath and make the air come from that region."

She pointed to her own underbelly. "Look, here it is!"

She drew in a deep breath and then exhaled. "Do you feel it? Normally, you breathe with your lungs. Now you should breathe with your underbelly. When singing the Beijing opera, you should direct your breath controlled by the diaphragm."

An followed her example and practiced breathing in this way.

"Master Xiang," he said with a smile, "I remember my biology teacher told us that human beings breathe with their lungs. I'm puzzled since there are only large intestines and caecum in my underbelly, how can I breathe like that? Would you please explain that to me?"

Yijun recalled the days when she learned the traditional operas from her father. She was so focused that she dared not make a stir or even sneeze. Alas, her present pupil even joked in a comical way in her presence. Yijun thought it was not the right way to learn the Beijing opera from your master. She felt displeased and cast a stare at him. On second thought, she blamed herself for being too serious because her pupil was learning the Beijing opera only for fun.

"You can continue to breathe with your lungs."

Yijun said flatly. "As you've learned how to sing the aria *Su San Being Sent Away under Escort*, let's select another aria. What about *Capture the Weihu Mountain by Stratagem*?"

Bai Wenli sent a car to fetch Xiang Hai for the lecture. When the chauffeur rang the doorbell, Xiang Hai had just finished ironing his clothes. He originally planned to wear a Zhongshan suit. After ironing the suit, he found a hole in the sleeve of the suit. He did not know when and how the hole got there. He took out a western suit and quickly ironed it. After he put on the suit, he followed the chauffeur downstairs. He stood beside the car and waited for the chauffeur to open the car door. To his surprise, the chauffeur got directly into the driver's seat. Xiang Hai was stunned by his impoliteness. He had to open the door himself and got into the car.

Since the school building was new, the windowpanes, desks, and chairs of the classroom were brand new also. When he entered the classroom, he saw it was more than half full. All the students fastened their eyes on him. Xiang Hai was a little nervous. "Good morning, everybody! I'd like to introduce myself. My name is Xiang Hai. Let's begin the class."

Xiang Hai was teaching the aria *Farewell My Concubine*. He sang the following lines first:

"Ever since I accompanied the king in fighting east and west / I've suffered cold weather and hardship year after year / I hate the State of Qin for plunging people into the abyss of untold suffering / The common people have to wander about homeless and penniless / When I saw the king sleeping soundly in the tent / I walked out of the tent for a stroll / I'm moving softly and halted my steps in the wilderness / I raised my head to see a clear and bright moon in the sky / I've heard the soldiers discussing widely / Revealing their sinking morale and divided loyalty—"

As Xiang Hai had not sung the Beijing opera in public for a long time, fine sweat broke out on his forehead. After he finished singing, he gazed at the audience and found the students motionless. Xiang Hai was disappointed. All of a sudden, the jolly ringing of a cell phone came from the corner of the classroom. A girl holding the cell phone rushed out of the room. A moment later she came back and sat down on her seat without saying anything to Xiang Hai. Xiang Hai was dumbfounded by the sound of her high-heeled shoes.

His first lecture was a complete failure. Cell phones were ringing from time to time. Some students went out to talk on their phones and some others rushed out to the restroom. They paid no heed to the presence of their teacher. A male student sitting at the back row was chewing gum. Putting his hands in his pockets and reclining his body against the back of the chair, he was rotating the gum in his mouth in a skillful way while staring at Xiang Hai. A female student sitting at the front row was reading a magazine right before his eyes. She ignored all the others and noisily turned the pages. Xiang Hai was puzzled and tried to scold her with a few well-chosen words. Before he opened his mouth, the girl student looked up and smiled at him. An instant later, she bent down to continue to read her magazine.

Xiang Hai did not utter a word. He was bewildered. Was this a common phenomenon nowadays in the classroom? Without entering a classroom for decades, he found it difficult to explain what he had seen.

When the class was over, Xiang Hai half rose from his seat, saying to the students, "That's all for today." He slowly picked up his lecture notes. He was demure as a maiden while the students were quick as rabbits. After a couple of minutes, all of them left and only Xiang Hai stayed.

The chauffeur told Xiang Hai that the car was out of order and he could not drive him home. "You can take the school's shuttle bus. The destination is the People's Square." With a cigarette between his lips, the chauffeur pointed to the entrance of the school. "Well, there it is."

Xiang Hai walked to the entrance and got on the shuttle bus. All the seats were occupied. Only a few people stood on the bus while the seated students were chatting merrily. Even some students who had just listened to his lecture did not greet him. Xiang Hai chose a vacant place and stood there with one hand holding his briefcase and the other hand grabbing the overhead baggage rack. When the bus started to move, Xiang Hai failed to grab tightly the rack and fell backwards. The man who stood behind him caught hold of him.

"Thank you." Xiang Hai grabbed again the

baggage rack and tightly this time.

"Master Xiang, give me your briefcase," said one student sitting on the aisle seat. Xiang Hai looked in his direction and saw the male student who was chewing the gum in the classroom. He reached out his hand and to take Xiang Hai's briefcase.

"This particular shuttle buss run is the most crowded and there are always people without seats. Are you tired, Master Xiang?" asked the male student who was still chewing his gum.

"I'm OK." Xiang Hai thought he would offer his seat to him. To his surprise, the student had no intention to give up his seat. Xiang Hai regretted not to have said he was very tired. On second thought, he had nothing more to desire because this was the only student who offered to carry his briefcase. It was really a praiseworthy and generous act.

As there was no traffic jam, the shuttle bus reached the People's Square within 30 minutes. Xiang Hai took his briefcase from the male student and thanked him. He got off the bus and changed to the Metro. He got back home very fast.

Xiang Hai entered through the outer door and was almost knocked down by somebody rushing down the stairs. He steadied himself and saw the young man was already a dozen meters away.

"You little rascal, come back home right now!" An old woman was screaming over Xiang Hai's head. The woman on the fifth floor looked ashamed when she saw him. "Master Xiang, you are back." Then she quickly hid her face behind the window.

This woman was the only actress in the Beijing opera troupe who played the Qiu-style male painted-face role. She had a very promising career during that period. Later, she joined her husband in speculating in the stock market. She turned her focus to making money and did not give up until she lost all the family belongings. She neglected her performing career. Now, she could only make ends meet with a meager salary. Xiang Hai had easily figured out what the commotion was about. She behaved so awkwardly because her son probably stole some money from home to gamble with. He heaved a long sigh and walked upstairs slowly.

"Master Xiang," said a soft voice.

Xiang Hai raised his head only to see Luo Manjuan standing in front of him, holding a bowl of wontons in her hands. She fixed her eyes on him. "I made these wontons with shrimp filling. I hope you'll like it."

"Oh!" Xiang Hai quickly put down his briefcase and took the bowl of wonton with both hands. "I don't know how to thank you!" He was about to unlock the door when he found his hands were fully occupied. He was unable to get out the key.

Luo Manjuan gave him a gentle smile and took the bowl of wontons. "Please open the door first."

Xiang Hai cracked a smile to hide his awkward expression. "Come on in, please. I bought some high-class pu'er tea yesterday. Please come in and have a cup of tea."

Luo Manjuan declined his invitation. "No, thank you. I haven't brought in laundry yet. And my child will be back from school. I have to cook."

Xiang Hai did not want to give up. He fastened his eyes on her. "Well, it won't take you long to finish a cup of tea."

"OK, I'll have tea with you."

Xiang Hai brewed a cup of strong pu'er tea and brought it to her. Luo Manjuan sat there looking at the photos on the side table. Some were photos of Xiang Hai and his daughter and some others were photos of Xiang Hai in stage costume.

"Master Xiang, you haven't changed much and you're still in good shape," Luo Manjuan said.

Xiang Hai smiled. "I'm flattered. I'm so old that even an iron can't smooth my wrinkled face. Here's your tea."

Luo Manjuan took the cup of tea and put it down on the side table. She cast a glance at Xiang Hai, paused, and abruptly said, "Master Xiang, my son Xiaowei got into trouble in school yesterday." She was on the verge of tears.

Xiang Hai was shocked at first but recovered quickly. "What happened?"

"He got into a fight with his classmate and broke the boy's head. The wound had be sewn up with a dozen of stitches. The principal told me that the school will record a serious demerit for his fault. I know three serious demerits will result in dropout. Master Xiang, what can I do about it?" She was about to cry again.

Xiang Hai tried to comfort her. "It's nothing unusual for children to fight. Boys are boys. They are naughty by nature. Your son will behave himself when he grows up. You don't need to worry too much."

Luo Manjuan shook her head. "You don't know how naughty my son is. If I don't discipline him now, he will become as wicked as that good for nothing on the fifth floor."

It was the first time that Luo Manjuan had talked to Xiang Hai about her family. He did not expect her to talk trivialities like that in front of him. She could chitchat with women living in the same building. Any woman would be a much better listener than him. When he saw her eyes dropping to her lap and the tip of her nose trembling, he felt sorry for her. He thought it might seem more intimate to start their conversation with domestic chitchat.

"In nine cases out of ten, things do not turn out as one wishes. As for raising one's child, one can only do one's best—" He hesitated because he wondered whether he had made appropriate remarks. "Well, boys tend to start to understand things at a later age than girls. But when they reach the age of fifteen or sixteen, they may become enlightened overnight."

Luo Manjuan uttered a noncommittal sound. "To me, your daughter Yijun is the type I like most. She is serene and obedient. She has a good job and even knows how to sing traditional operas. How did you raise your daughter so well, Master Xiang? You must share your insights with me when you have time."

Xiang Hai flashed her a smile. "I know nothing about raising a child. My daughter is as stubborn as I am. I don't think such a temperament will be good for her in the present society." He presented the cup of tea to her. "Have some tea, please."

Luo Manjuan took a sip. "It's so fragrant. It must be very expensive."

"Not very."

Luo Manjuan did not stay long before she said goodbye. Xiang Hai walked her to the door. Only after she closed the door did he come back to his own apartment. When he cleaned the side table, he took the cup Luo Manjuan had used and saw a faint lipstick print on its rim. To his surprise, Luo Manjuan was a woman who made herself up instead of a plain one without adornment.

Xiang Hai recalled the dialogues between them. He had been very careful about his diction for fear of offending her or embarrassing himself. He thought over their conversation again and again. He could not help but laugh at himself for being as stupid as a lovesick boy. He found all the leading male characters in traditional operas were utterly stupid when they were infatuated, such as Zhang Junrui and Liu Mengmei. To be more exact, they were obsessed instead of being stupid. Following this line of thought, he found his face flushed. That was not because he was shy. He had a faint sense of excitement. He felt as if some sentiment in his heart was bubbling and rippling up almost to overflowing.

4

The section director gave Yijun a dressing-down. According to the customs regulations airport personnel were not allowed to buy cigarettes, wine, or cosmetics at the duty-free shops at the airport. When she was on duty, Yijun caught an airport employee buying duty-free cigarettes. It so happened that this man was the deputy commander of the command post. The section director ordered Yijun to return the cigarettes to the deputy commander. "Why did you have to catch him instead of somebody else?" the section director said bitterly.

Yijun was not convinced. Since there was no name written on his face, how could she know that he was the deputy commander? Besides, the customs regulations should apply to all people. Why should officials be an exception? Yijun was burdened with anxiety these days. She did not speak to the section director. She was stubborn and never concealed her true feelings. The section director did not take it seriously because she was a girl. The young woman sitting opposite to Yijun was called Ding Meimei. At the age of twenty-seven, the thin and tall woman was good at ballroom dancing. Big bosses liked to dance with her and brought her with them on many great occasions. As a result, she received special favors from them. Many colleagues guessed that she would be promoted when a new leader came. Ding Meimei was not on familiar terms with Yijun. But that day she even gave the director an accusing glance and said to Yijun in private, "Ignore that ass kisser!"

Yijun was dumbfounded by her remark. She thought carefully and found the answer. If she were the darling of big bosses like Ding Meimei, she would naturally take no notice of the section director. She would act as she wished. At the thought of this, Yijun regretted not having learned to dance.

Her uncle set her up on another date. His parents owned a restaurant. He worked as a salesman at a toy company after his graduation from university.

"Don't tell him that you like to sing traditional operas," her uncle reminded her again and again before their first date.

"Why?"

Her uncle knitted his brows. "Just do it the way I told you. Why should you tell him about your hobby since this is not an interview conducted by the Beijing opera troupe?"

They met at McDonald's. Zhao Xilin was the young man's name. He was medium in stature and wore glasses.

"What are your hobbies?" Xilin asked after they had been chatting for a while.

"Singing the Beijing opera."

When she recalled her uncle's exhortation, she stuck out her tongue in private. Xilin was puzzled by her expression. "What's wrong?"

"Nothing," Yijun said quickly. "What are your hobbies?"

"I like to play cards," Xilin answered without

thinking. "I'm good at all kinds of card games."

"Do you like to watch the traditional operas?" Yijun asked.

Xilin shook his head. "I don't like it because I don't understand the lines. Do you like it? I'm surprised there're still young people who like to watch the Beijing opera."

Yijun found his candid attitude amusing. "Aside from watching the Beijing opera, I like to sing its arias."

When she raised her head, Yijun saw An passing by the window. He was accompanied by a girl in her early twenties. The girl had shoulder-length hair. Her silhouette showed she had delicate features. Yijun thought the girl would be Yu Feifei. Before she had a good look at her, she had walked away.

Yijun lowered her head and sipped the fruit juice in her glass. Xilin cast a stare at her. "My mother likes to watch traditional operas," he said. "And she also sings the arias of *Red Mansions* and *Desert Prince*. Her singing is quite pleasant."

Yijun smiled. "That's the Shaoxing opera. I only know how to sing the Beijing opera."

"They are both traditional operas nonetheless,"

Xilin said.

Yijun cracked another smile.

Xilin glanced at her and hesitated briefly. "How about joining me in a card game when you're free next week?"

On the weekend, An came for his Beijing opera lesson with Yijun. He was in a sullen mood. He kept silent most of the time. Yijun wanted to ask him about seeing him outside McDonald's, but she reeled in her curiosity when she saw his bad mood.

"Do you know how to sing *The Peony Pavilion*?" An asked.

"I'm not good at singing the Kunqu opera. I've learned only a few lines."

An took out a cigarette and lit it. "Would you please sing an aria for me?"

Yijun hesitated a bit before she agreed to his request.

"What a riot of brilliant purple and tender crimson / Among the ruined wells and crumbling walls / What an enchanting sight on this fine morning / Whose is this courtyard where people can enjoy themselves—"

After she finished singing, she saw An staring at her with a blank expression. He stood still and seemed in a daze. "What's wrong with you?" She said, waving her hand in front of his face. "You don't feel well?"

"Yes, I do feel unwell." He replied, pointing at his heart. "I feel unwell here. I have an unbearable pain."

"Do you have a stomachache?" Yijun asked. "Should I take you to the hospital?"

An cast a glance at her. "For a performing artist, how can you be so flat and plain. Is this my stomach? No, it's my heart! Listen to me. I have a heartache. A serious one."

Yijun looked at him, cracked a smile, and said nothing.

An let out a heavy sigh. "Your singing was fantastic. It's the first time that I've felt the singing of traditional operas can be so pleasant to the ear. I don't know how to describe my feeling. Your singing penetrated my heart. I felt as if a pair of hands pulled me into it. I've come to realize why the older generation is so fond of traditional operas. They have their reasons. Well, to be frank, I believe I'm convinced." He ended his remark with an emphatic nod.

Then An told Yijun that he had broken up with Yu Feifei.

"It can't be called a breakup because in a sense she has never been my girlfriend." A mirthless smile flickered across his face. "I courted her assiduously for the whole year, but she never take me seriously. I knew very well what she was thinking. How can she take a mere nobody as her boyfriend? She's such a good catch that she can pick up a much better boyfriend than me." He drew a deep inhale from his cigarette and then turned his head to look outward through the window.

A lock of hair over An's temple was grayish and brilliant, maybe the result of sunshine. With his hands in his pants pockets, he looked out the window and moved his lips as though he was muttering to himself.

"Listen to me. There is no lack of virtuous and talented girls on earth," Yijun paused and laughed at herself for making such a ridiculous remark. Then she smiled and continued. "Do you still want to learn the opera? If you like *The Peony Pavilion*, I can teach you to sing this aria."

An gave her a faint smile. "That'll be nice, but

this aria is too difficult to learn. I'm afraid it's beyond me."

"It doesn't matter. I can teach you several times. Since I have enough patience to teach you, why should you lose confidence yourself?" As soon as she finished her talk, she took out two long sleeves from her handbag as if she was a magician conjuring a trick. "Come and put these on."

An stared at her. "What are you doing?"

"These are theatrical long sleeves," Yijun explained as she helped him put on the sleeves. "With them on you'll feel as if you are giving a performance. When you fix your eyes on here, you should wave your sleeve to that side. Make the expression in your eyes more winsome."

"Please get them off me!" An yelled. "I don't want to look like a sissy."

"Don't worry, you're far from being sissy." Yijun grinned before snatching his cigarette to throw it into the ash can. "Don't smoke anymore. Smoking will damage your voice. My dad seldom smokes. If you want to learn the traditional opera from me, you must quit smoking."

An cracked a smile and cast a glance at her. He

was about to say something, but he kept himself under control. "OK, as you're my master, I'll listen to you." He waved the two long sleeves and burst into laughter. "If my clients see me like this, I can assure you none of them dare buy insurance policies from me anymore!"

Bai Wenli had become extremely busy. In addition to his routine work at the school and troupe, he was cast in two TV series and rehearsing for a play. He was not afraid of working round the clock. What tormented him most was the trouble Yu Feifei had got him into. Yu Feifei called him several times recommending herself for the leading female role in the movie version of the Kunqu opera *The Peony Pavilion*. This movie was financed by a Hong Kong boss. With the introduction of his friend, Bai Wenli had two meals together with the Hong Kong boss. For the sake of courtesy the boss asked him to recommend some actors and actresses. As soon as she got wind of this, Yu Feifei fastened onto him like a leech. She employed both soft and hard tactics to seek his help. It seemed to him that she would never give up until her goal was achieved.

A year earlier Bai Wenli led the troupe on a performing tour to Singapore. During the tour Yu Feifei knocked on the door of his room and jumped into his bed. Whenever he recalled the incident, he regretted having slept with her. Yu Feifei was a beauty as well as an excellent actress. Naturally, he recommended her to play the second leading female role in the most important play for the next year. Quite a few people in the troupe objected to his proposal. Was it appropriate for a girl actress who had just graduated from school to play such an important role? Bai Wenli firmly supported Yu Feifei. Finally, the head of the troupe accepted his proposal. Her performance was quite a success. In this way, Yu Feifei became one of the best young *huadan* actresses in the troupe.

Bai Wenli did not expect that Yu Feifei's desire was insatiable. Now she even wanted to be cast for a leading female role in a movie. He turned down her request. She said nothing at first. However, two days later she sent a photo to him via email. Bai Wenli was frightened out of his wits. The photo was of them having sex. Now Bai Wenli knew how vicious and merciless this girl was. He immediately called her to tell her that he would arrange an appointment for her to meet the Hong Kong boss. It would be her responsibility to secure a deal.

"Thank you very much, Master Bai." Yu Feifei's voice on the phone was soft and coquettish. "It's very kind of you!"

Bai Wenli wiped the sweat from his forehead. He was about to take a bath when the phone rang. It was Xiang Hai calling.

"I've been feeling under the weather lately," Xiang Hai said. "You'd better ask someone better qualified to give the lectures."

Bai Wenli was irritated by Xiang Hai's request. But he managed to control his temper. "My senior co-learner, you're making things difficult for me. As you know, many students attend lectures simply because they admire your fame. If you leave, who else will be able to attract them? Please do me a favor by finishing this semester, OK? I can increase your lecture fee by 10%."

"It has nothing to do with money," Xiang Hai said.

"I know you don't think much of money. Besides, you're not lacking in pocket money, but my senior co-learner, please, I'm begging you!"

Bai Wenli put down the phone and uttered a sound of contempt. That day the chauffeur told him that he did not drive Xiang Hai home because the car broke down he knew immediately that Xiang Hai would be offended. After he learned from several students what had happened at the lecture, he was well aware that Xiang Hai would take it to heart. Xiang Hai was good at singing arias, nevertheless he was not a famous actor. Because of that, the snobbish students would not show much respect to him. Xiang Hai's call was what Bai Wenli had anticipated.

"Why should you ask him to give lectures?" Bai Wenli's wife said. "He doesn't know how to take a proper measure of himself. If you beg him like this, he will imagine himself a top-class teacher without whom the school will be unable to exist."

Bai Wenli kept silent.

She curled her lips and continued. "Such a fat lecture fee will attract any teacher. Why should you stick to this ungrateful fool?"

"I don't think you're being fair," Bai Wenli said. "He is capable in many ways."

"What is he capable of? I know your field very

well. The performers of the Beijing opera are skilled workers. Any fool can learn how to sing some arias if he practices every day. As he hasn't appeared on the stage for a long time, I really don't know what he's capable of now."

Bai Wenli knitted his brows. On the excuse of smoking, he went out to the balcony. He stood still for a while. He did not light his cigarette. Leaning on the rail, he looked off into the distance. The school days when he and Xiang Hai learned the traditional operas were vivid in his memory. They were both in their early twenties at that time. They would start to exercise their voice at dawn. Afterwards they practiced the basic skills of the Beijing opera. At that time a girl student always kept them company. She was fond of smiling. Every time she smiled, her eyes would shape like a crescent moon. She was fond of the Xun-style roles and liked very much to sing *Selling Water*: "I look at myself in the mirror after I get up early in the morning / I do my hair with osmanthus-scented pomade / I paint my face by putting on peach-blossom powder / I apply apricot-pink rouge to my lips." Later she became Xiang Hai's wife. She died not long after Yijun was born.

Bai Wenli still remembered the days when she was hospitalized. When Bai Wenli visited her in the hospital, she would say to him in a serious manner: "My husband Xiang Hai knows nothing except performing traditional operas. I hope you'll take good care of him after I die." Bai Wenli could only forced a faint smile.

After she passed away, Xiang Hai who had never drunk was intoxicated from wine for several months. He drank down his sorrow every day. He refused to attend rehearsals or give performances. Gradually he ruined his career. He was not open to anyone's persuasion.

Bai Wenli put a cigarette between his lips and lit it. He puffed away to the sky.

Bursts of laughter kept ringing in his ear. He knew nobody was laughing nearby. He had such a hallucination simply because he cherished the memory of somebody. He also knew that he had invited Xiang Hai to give lectures simply because of somebody's last words. In the last few years, many people had proposed to suspend Xiang Hai's salary, but he tried every effort to turn down their proposal. Xiang Hai had no idea what had happened. He did not care whether Xiang Hai had learned the truth, because he did not do these things for his sake.

After putting down the phone, Xiang Hai went online and started to chat with Liu Mengmei.

"He said many students attended lectures simply because they admired my fame. I know he was appeasing me. I'm not a famous performer like Mei Lanfang. How could they admire me?" Xiang cracked a wry smile.

"Is there any progress in your relationship with the woman next door?" Liu Mengmei seemed very interested in this matter. He never forgot to mention this in his chat. If this was a face-to-face chat, Xiang Hai would never talk about this. As this was an online, no restrictions of any kind were imposed because no one knew with whom you were chatting. Anyway, he wanted to have a good listener so that he could bare his thoughts. That was why he told him everything in detail.

"The other day she offered me a bowl of homemade wontons. I asked her to come to my home and have a cup of tea. We chatted for a while."

"What did you talk about?" Liu Mengmei asked.

"Nothing special. We engaged in casual chitchat only."

"Since she took the initiative, does it mean she took a fancy to you?"

Xiang Hai's heart leapt when he read this. "I don't know. I don't dare to guess. I'd rather she didn't know my true feelings. I hope our relationship will remain as a riddle. Do you think I'm silly, Liu Mengmei?"

"Somebody else may laugh at you for being silly. I won't. I know you very well," Liu Mengmei said. "It'll be interesting to keep it secret. Just like acting on the stage, you cast a glance at me and I steal a glance at you. In this way we don't bare our thoughts in words. Even if we talk with each other, we only utter a few words. This kind of situation will leave a prolong impact, don't you think so?"

Xiang Hai meditated on these words and had to admit that Liu Mengmei almost read his thoughts. He felt embarrassed. "Who are you, Liu Mengmei? I no longer think you're a young man. You work in artistic circles, don't you?"

Liu Mengmei posted the sign of a smiling face on the screen. "I'm not going to tell you. If you know the truth, it won't be amusing anymore."

Xiang Hai also posted a smiling face on the screen. He learned this technique from Liu Mengmei, who told him to single click the signs on the animation bar.

"Is that woman beautiful?" Liu Mengmei asked abruptly.

Xiang Hai thought it over. "Not beautiful, but pleasant looking."

"How did you take a fancy to her?"

Xiang Hai hesitated for a while before replying. "Because she looks like my late wife."

An did not meet Yijun for two weeks. His absence was something she had expected. Yijun did not take it seriously. An started to learn the Beijing opera for the sole purpose of courting a girl. And now that they had broken up, he did not need to learn from her anymore. Yijun still went to the school at the appointed time once every week. She would stay there for half an hour. If he failed to show up, she would go back home. She did not call him for fear of hurting his feelings. It was out of her expectations that he appeared in front of her on the third weekend, smiling.

"Master Xiang, how're you doing?" An said while eating a hamburger. "I rushed here as soon as I signed a policy with a client. You look good. You haven't changed at all."

Yijun stared at him and tried to put on a grave expression. But on second thought, she gave up the idea of frightening him. Instead, she smiled at him. "You look good yourself. You haven't changed either."

An felt embarrassed. "I thought you would not be here. I'm sorry. I forgot to call you on the previous two occasions. Forgive me for keeping you waiting and wasting your time."

Yijun shrugged her shoulders. "Forget about it. A trip here is like a stroll for me. It's not far from my home."

"Let me treat you to a dinner tonight," An said. "Please accept my apology." Yijun cracked a smile. "That'll be nice. It so happens that my dad went to visit his old classmate and there is nobody cooking for me."

An said he would continue to learn *The Peony Pavilion* from her. Yijun looked surprised at his remark. An scratched his head with embarrassment. "So...we make up again."

Yijun cursed her slow-wittedness. She should have known. "Congratulations!" Yijun said. Seeing his face glow with happiness, she could not but feel a little bit disappointed. It was a sudden thing that flashed across her mind and she did not give it serious thought. She smiled at him and took out a stage costume. She took the stage costume without her father's knowledge. Though she did not expect him to appear today, she still brought the stage costume with her. At the thought of this, she found her behavior strange. She was not mad at him for being absent without reason for two weeks. She was delighted to see him again.

With a broad smile, An put on the stage costume and waved the long sleeves. "With all the props ready, I'm all the more anxious to learn."

An looked funny when he learned the Kunqu opera. His mouth curled, his brows lifted, and his eyes moved closer until they were crossed. All his limbs moved mechanically like a puppet. Yijun watched carefully. She did not laugh at him because she knew he was trying his best. She taught him how to display the orchid-shaped fingers. There should be a good coordination between his eyes and his nose, and between his nose and his heart. His eyes should follow the movement of his hand.

An practiced good-naturedly with a smile.

"There's nothing to laugh at. Performing a traditional opera is like this," Yijun said. "Remember right now you are Du Liniang. As you are a daughter from a family of good social standing and your parents have brought you up under stern discipline, you have to stay indoors all the time. It's a rare chance for you to tour the garden. When you see the beautiful scenery in the garden, you feel you've wasted your youthful years. As a result, all sorts of emotions are surging up within you. You should put yourself in her place and share her feelings. Only in this way can you act with a natural expression, look, and movement, and achieve the desired results."

An took her advice and imitated her carefully. He followed her in singing every line and making every movement. When she turned around, he also turned around. Due to his clumsiness, he almost bumped into her. She corrected his movement. "You should turn around like this." She gave him another demonstration. He still failed in his practice. She taught him how to turn around by holding his arms with one hand and embracing his waist lightly with the other hand. "You move your head, then your eyes, then shoulders, and finally your waist. Slowly... slowly..."

An followed her instruction obediently and made some progress. Yijun nodded her head. "It seems you've learned the rudiments." She loosened her grip and saw him smiling at her. Carried away by emotion, she returned his smile.

"I find I've come to understand something," An said suddenly after practicing for a while.

"What do you understand?" Yijun asked.

"I understand the feelings of the play. I can't tell you exactly. It's strange that as soon as I put on the stage costume, I came to understand something." He paused and then continued. "It's really interesting to perform the traditional opera."

Yijun nodded her head. She was going to say a few encouraging words when she changed her mind suddenly. Instead, she said, "When you get married with your girlfriend and achieve your purpose, you'll give up learning the traditional opera for sure." The minute she uttered these words, she found her remarks neither here nor there. In embarrassment she cast a glance at An and said, "I know you have only a short-lived zeal."

An shook his head and smiled at her. "That's not true. To tell you the truth, I'm very fond of singing the traditional operas now. I know you want me to beat a retreat so that I won't bother you every week."

Yijun averted her eyes from his face. "Well, I don't mind. If you are interested, you can go on learning. If you want to give it up, I have no objection. Anyway, I've gained nothing out of this." Suddenly she realized she had made an inappropriate remark. She blamed herself for making one slip of the tongue after another.

"Oh, I'm being too thoughtless," An said immediately. "Master Xiang, I'll give you a gift. What kind of gift do you like?"

Yijun was nonplussed. "I like nothing. Don't buy anything for me!"

As soon as she realized her tone was too harsh, her face flushed with embarrassment. She lowered her head and feigned as if she was smoothing out her bangs. "I'm hungry. Let's go eat."

An glanced at his watch. "It's not yet four o'clock.

Are you sure you're hungry?" She gave a reassuring nod. "Yes. I don't know why I feel hungry at such an early hour. Do you think it's weird?"

5

In the morning Xiang Hai was hanging the laundry on the balcony. He was slow in motion. He was clipping every piece of clothing in a deliberately slow manner. He stole a glance at Luo Manjuan's balcony from time to time. He surmised that it was about time for her to hang her laundry. After finishing his job, Xiang Hai started to water the flowers. It did not take long for him to finish watering all the flowers. He thought he might go inside his apartment first and come out again when she appeared. On second thought, he was afraid that she might see through his real motive. He decided to stay on the balcony waiting for her to appear. He pretended to do physical exercises by stretching his legs and swaying his waist.

Ten minutes later, Luo Manjuan came out. Instead of hanging the laundry, she hung out some sausages, salted pork, and soy sauce braised beef. Xiang

Hai started the conversation. "Good morning!"

Lu Manjuan looked up. "Good morning!"

"Why have you prepared so much salted food?" Xiang Hai asked.

"My son likes salted food," she answered. "I'm afraid I started preparations this year later than usual. I wonder whether the food will be ready for the Spring Festival."

Xiang Hai had two tickets in his pocket. These tickets were given by the troupe for the performance of the highlights from *laosheng*-centered Beijing operas. He cast a glance at her and tried to figure out how to invite her. As he was undecided, he had to spend time arranging the flowers and pruning the twigs. He stole a glance at her for fear that she might go back to her room any time.

After a prolonged hesitation, he managed to say in a casual manner, "Yesterday my troupe gave me two tickets," he finally managed to say in a casual manner after a prolonged hesitation. "I was going to go with Yijun. Unfortunately, she won't be free that day. I'm afraid these tickets will be wasted."

Then he flashed her a smile.

"Master Xiang, you can go by yourself," Luo

Manjuan said.

"I will be really bored if I have to watch the performance alone. I'm afraid I have to waste them."

As soon as Xiang Hai uttered this remark, he found he had made an error and left no room for maneuver.

"On Friday my worthless son will go to his classmate's birthday party. I'll be left alone at home," Luo Manjuan said as she fixed her eyes on him. "Master Xiang, I'm also a fan of the Beijing opera. Can I go to the theatre with you? Why should you waste your tickets?"

Xiang Hai was so surprised and delighted that he would have liked to shout for joy. He tried his best to suppress his emotion. "That's a good idea," he said calmly. "As we're neighbors, we can go and come back together and chat to kill time."

"You're right." With a smile, Luo Manjuan went into her apartment.

Xiang Hai went back into his apartment. In hindsight, he felt he had used a too cold tone. It was not easy for a woman like Luo Manjuan to offer to keep him company. However, he had adopted an indifferent attitude toward the matter. His remark must have embarrassed her. It was irrational for him to overact.

Xiang Hai took out a purple brooch from the drawer. The shell-shaped brooch was extended outward and looked like a branch. Yijun had bought this unique brooch. But later she thought it was old-fashioned and wanted to return it to the shop. Xiang Hai liked it and took it from his daughter, saying he might use it as a gift. He planned to give it to Luo Manjuan when they went to the theatre together. He thought this elegant brooch would suit her. A faint smile flickered across his face when he imagined how she would look when she wore the brooch.

On Friday Xiang Hai and Luo Manjuan set out after supper. Clad in a dark reddish purple overcoat and a grey wool skirt, Luo Manjuan put her permed hair into a bun. She was holding a light brown purse.

Xiang Hai looked at her admiringly. "You're beautiful."

Luo Manjuan felt a bit shy. "Master Xiang, I'm flattered."

Staring at her dark reddish purple overcoat, Xiang Hai thought the brooch was a perfect match for it.

There was a traffic jam so they reached the theatre only a few minutes before the performance began. Xiang Hai knew the majority of the leading actors because they entered the troupe almost at the same time. Tonight's program included some highlights of the *laosheng*-centered repertoires. *Laosheng's* singing was so melodious that the performance attracted a large audience. The theatre almost had a full house. Xiang Hai stole glances at Luo Manjuan from time to time. She fixed her eyes on the stage and enjoyed the performance very much. Xiang Hai was amused by her full attention. He patted her on the shoulder and asked her whether she'd like a drink. She shook her hand. "No, thank you."

After the performance was over, they waited on the curb for a passing taxi, but none came for a long time.

"We may as well take a bus," Luo Manjuan said. "It'll save money and won't take much longer for us to get home."

Xiang Hai agreed because in this way he could stay with her for a longer time. They walked to the bus stop and the bus came quickly. It so happened there were two vacant seats with one in front of the other.

So Xiang Hai sat behind Luo Manjuan.

As it was dark outside, the bus window became a mirror reflecting the passengers inside. Xiang Hai saw Luo Manjuan take out her cell phone from her purse. It seemed she was texting a message. After she put the cell phone back, she took out her compact and applied some powder on her face. Amused by her behavior, Xiang Hai thought to himself: a woman is a woman. She will never forget to touch up her makeup even though she would be home in a few minutes.

They got off the bus and walked slowly toward their house.

"The wind is blowing at night," Xiang Hai said. "Do you feel cold?"

"Not very." Luo Manjuan replied.

"Thank you for keeping me company tonight."

Luo Manjuan gave him a faint smile. "It's me who should thank you because you treated me to such a wonderful performance."

Xiang Hai smiled. "It's not my treat. The tickets were given by the troupe. It's a favor done at no cost to myself."

He put his hand into his pocket and thought hard as to when he should give her the brooch. He was afraid his blunt behavior might embarrass them both if she refused to accept the gift. Swayed by considerations of gain and loss, they reached their homes before he knew it. Luo Manjuan opened the burglarproof door with her key and looked up at her apartment. "I wonder whether my son has come back. There's no light on. He must have had a great time at the party and forgotten to come back home."

Xiang Hai replied in a noncommittal manner and started to climb up the stairs. All of a sudden, he heard a ringing voice: "Mom!" He turned his head and saw it was Luo Manjuan's son Xiaowei. With a bag slung over his shoulder, Xiaowei was holding a skewer of mutton cubes and his mouth was covered with grease. Xiang Hai hurriedly held the door open for him to get in.

"You're eating shish kebab again. How many times I have told you it's dirty. You should not eat it!" Luo Manjuan gave her son a dressing-down.

Xiaowei curled his lips. "I'm starving."

Luo Manjuan cast a glance at Xiang Hai. "How could it be? You didn't have supper, did you?"

Before Xiaowei got the chance to answer, Luo Manjuan pulled him upstairs. "Let's go home. Take a bath and go to bed right away. It's already late."

When he stopped at the door of his apartment, Xiang Hai knew it was impossible for him to give the brooch to Luo Manjuan. He felt a bit upset.

"Say good night to Uncle," Luo Manjuan told Xiaowei.

Xiaowei waved his hand. "Good night, Uncle."

Xiang Hai smiled at him. "Good night."

Luo Manjuan brought her son in. Before she shut the door, Xiang Hai heard her son complain: "The food at Granny's home was not inviting—" The door was completely shut.

Xiang Hai had a niggling doubt: did Xiaowei go to the party or to his Granny's home?

When he got into his room, Xiang Hai put the brooch back in the drawer. Then he pulled out the two ticket stubs and saw four words "For staff members only" were stamped on each ticket. A sudden thought flashed across his mind. Since Luo Manjuan was the wife of their former staff member, the troupe would certainly give her a ticket. Xiang Hai recalled in detail the situation. Before he told her when the performance would be put on, she said "On Friday my worthless son will go to his classmate's birthday party. I'll be left alone at home." No doubt she had gotten her ticket, otherwise she would not be able to know the performance would be given on Friday. Xiang Hai was in a daze. He did not expect things would turn out like that.

"Women are really unfathomable," Xiang Hai said to Liu Mengmei. "If I had known her intention, I would have invited her to go to the theatre together in a natural way. It would save a lot of guessing."

Liu Mengmei posted a smiling face on the screen. "Don't you like to keep your relationship with her neither warm nor cold? Don't you like the sentiment of distancing her so as to accept her? She probably knew your taste. That's why she liked to play with you in this way."

"I guess she likes you, too. Am I right?" Liu Mengmei asked after a brief pause.

"Perhaps," Xiang Hai answered.

"What if she wants to get married?" Liu Mengmei asked.

"I don't think she wants to marry me."

"That's hard to say."

Xiang Hai stared at these words blankly. He

could not tell whether he was shocked or he did not feel his usual self. He was utterly confused and disconcerted. Then he heard the knock at the door. Xiang Hai opened the door and saw Luo Manjuan standing there.

She was holding a bowl of steaming hot soup. "Chicken soup. I cooked the famous Jiangsu hen for the whole afternoon. I hope you'll like it." With a smile she handed the bowl of soup to Xiang Hai.

Xiang Hai looked at the yellowish chicken soup and took it after a brief hesitation. He did not act as quickly as when he took the bowl of wontons a few days earlier. Luo Manjuan sensed his hesitation, cast a glance at him and then said smilingly, "In the cold weather a hot bowl of nourishing chicken soup can help you keep warm."

"Thank you," Xiang Hai said.

He was still in a daze while holding the bowl of chicken soup. The hot soup burned his hand and he could not help uttering a sound.

"Put it on the table," Luo Manjuan said. "I've got to go." She walked to the door. She was closing the door when she saw Xiang Hai still looking at her. Slightly flushed, she flashed him a smile.

Seeing her flushed face, Xiang Hai felt his heart leap. He quickly shut the door. He walked to his computer and wanted to go continue with his net chat. To his disappointment, Liu Mengmei had gone offline.

Yijun was playing cards at Xilin's home. She hadn't felt like playing cards. But she did not wish to refuse him since he had invited her several times. Xilin came to fetch her and did not reveal his true motive until she got in the car. When she learned they were going to his home to play cards, she thought he was a person who always got his own way. But she did not allow herself to think too much of it because she had decided she would never play cards with him again.

His parents were kind to her. After a short conversation, Xilin got straight to the point. "Let's play cards!"

He, his parents, and Yijun made up the number for the card game "Fight against the Landlord." Yijun did not know how to play. Xilin showed her how to distinguish between the landlord and the peasant. His parents were smiling at her while listening to their son's instruction. Yijun learned the basic rules of the game, but she was not a good card player.

"If we had gambled with money," Xilin said to her after several rounds. "You would have been a big loser."

The TV was broadcasting the entertainment news. She listened to the anchorman's announcement: "The Kunqu opera *The Peony Pavilion* will soon be made into a film. It will be a theatrical film backed by a substantial investment. The young Beijing opera performer Yu Feifei will play the leading female role."

As soon as she heard this, Yijun turned to look at the TV and saw a very pretty girl in a figure hugging black dress on the screen smiling at the cameras. Yijun recognized her as the same girl who had passed by McDonald's with An.

"Since you're a Beijing opera performer, where did you get the idea of playing a role in a Kunqu opera film?" A reporter asked.

She gave a charming smile and smoothed back her long hair. "I learned the Kunqu opera when I was a student. So the Kunqu opera is in my line. What's more, the Beijing opera and the Kunqu opera are of the same family. Many Beijing opera performers are also good at singing the Kunqu opera."

Yu Feifei's voice was sweet and she had dimples when she smiled.

With her eyes glued on the screen, Yijun understood why An wanted to learn *The Peony Pavilion*. As she was absentminded, she played a wrong hand during the card game.

"Why didn't you pick acting as your career?" Xilin's mother asked her.

"I don't have a good voice," Yijun said casually. "I'm not qualified to be a professional actress. I'm just an amateur."

"It doesn't seem to be an interesting job," Xilin chirped in. "What's worse, it's hard and arduous work."

Yijun cast a stare at him and could not help refuting his argument. "You don't understand the fun of performing traditional operas. In fact, it's very interesting."

Xilin expressed his disapproval. "There're many interesting jobs. Why should one take this one? You see," he pointed at the TV screen, "even that opera performer wants to be a film star. Who else will be interested in traditional operas?"

After dinner, Xilin walked Yijun home. On the

way back Yijun intended to tell Xilin that it would be their last meeting. But she changed her mind for fear of embarrassing him and herself. She made up her mind to let him know the truth by phone.

After she got home, she took a bath and went to bed. She saw Yu Feifei's charming dimples again in her mind. The memories of An singing "What a riot of brilliant purple and tender crimson / Among the ruined wells and crumbling walls—" in a shrill voice flashed in her head. It was amusing and thought provoking. In the end she felt a bit distressed. Yijun turned off the light and sat up for a while in darkness. She suddenly pointed her orchid-shaped fingers at her own forehead, saying in a Beijing-opera tone, "You're really stupid." The last word "stupid" reverberated several rounds in the room. All of a sudden, her sentimental and lingering tone came to a dead stop.

After today's lecture, Xiang Hai found the chauffeur had loose bowels. He looked pale after paying several visits to the restroom. Xiang Hai offered to take the school bus home. When he got on the bus, all the seats had been occupied. He tried to find a place where he could stand.

"Master Xiang, take my seat." He heard somebody call to him.

It was the student who always chewed gum in class.

"Thank you," Xiang Hai said, trying to hide his surprise as he sat.

"Can I hold your bag for you?" Xiang Hai asked him.

"Don't bother," the student answered. "My bag is not heavy."

Xiang Hai watched him hang the bag around his neck and hold the overhead handrail with both his hands. He looked like a monkey playing on the swing.

"Where do you live?" Xiang Hai asked

"At Wujiaochang."

"That's quite far from the school."

"It's OK. After I get off the school bus, I only need to transfer twice," the student said as he chewed his gum loudly. "Master Xiang, where do you live?"

"In Pudong."

"You live even farther away."

Xiang Hai smiled. "It's a long distance, but it's convenient with the subway."

Xiang Hai was a bit tired and wanted to take a

short nap. But he thought it would be impolite not to talk with the student as he was standing by his side. The student started to talk about the Beijing opera. He said he started to like singing the Beijing opera when he was a child. Even when he passed the university entrance exam, he still decided to enroll himself at the traditional opera school. "My parents objected to my idea. They said, 'As a normal young man, why should you learn traditional operas?' But they were unable to bring me round. I said to them, 'If you don't let me learn the traditional operas, I'll work as a street cleaner.' They were so scared that they had to give up."

After they got off the school bus, they walked together for a few blocks. The student exchanged his cell phone number with Xiang Hai.

"Master Xiang, don't hesitate to call me if there is any physical job at home," the student said when they reached the subway station. "I know you have only a daughter. It's not easy for her to do physical labor."

Xiang Hai was moved by his remarks. "Thank you very much."

They kept on talking with each other for quite a while before they said goodbye.

Xiang Hai was in such a good mood that he hummed an aria as he climbed up the stairs. When he took out his key at the door, he stopped humming immediately because he was afraid Luo Manjuan might bring him another bowl of wontons or chicken soup. He tiptoed into his apartment as if he were a thief. He wondered why he should act like this in his own house.

Xilin invited Yijun to a movie with him and two other friends of his. They plan play cards after the movie. Yijun politely declined. She was about to explain after an initial hesitation, but he hung up the phone. She had no chance to make an excuse.

After work, someone proposed to go to a hotpot restaurant to celebrate a colleague's birthday. A dozen of colleagues went to this party. Only Ding Meimei excused herself by saying there was something urgent to deal with at home. While enjoying the meal, they talked about the reshuffle of the present leading group. As the present general manager was moved and reduced to a lower rank for some unexplained reason, Ding Meimei did not benefit from it. Since she was not even promoted to the rank of deputy section chief, it was only natural that she was in a gloomy mood. There were rumors that the new general manager was not interested in dancing at all.

"This time there is no longer any hope for Ding Meimei," someone said. "She will be completely out of favor with the new leader."

"I wonder what hobby the new leader is pursuing. If I learn the truth, I'll take up his pet hobby right away," one colleague said jokingly.

"If he likes to play golf and attend the western grand opera, you'll have to bear considerable expenses," another colleague said.

"No matter how much it costs you, you'll go with it because your rapid promotion in the rest of your life will depend on it."

Yijun did not take part in their gossiping. While listening to them, she constantly dipped the mutton slices into the pot. Then she picked up the boiled ones and put them in her neighbors' bowls. Ms. Gu, who sat next to her, was the oldest in their section. She was warmhearted and offered to find a date for her. Yijun cracked a noncommittal smile.

"What type do you like?" Ms. Gu asked her.

"Anyone I can get along well with," She answered and then added with a smile, "It'll be more ideal if he likes to sing the Beijing opera."

Ms. Gu uttered a sound of surprise. "Well, I'm afraid it's not easy to find someone like that."

After they finished their meal, Yijun took a taxi home. On the way, her cell phone rang. It was An calling. He spoke in a noisy background. "I want to go to karaoke. Do you want to join me?"

Yijun was in a daze.

"I'll be at Luwan Karaoke Club," An said. "Are you going to come?"

"How many people will be there?" Yijun asked.

"Just you and me."

Yijun was in a daze again. "I'll come."

Half an hour later Yijun arrived at the karaoke club. She found An in a reserved room sitting languidly on the couch. He was singing at the top of his lungs the popular song "The Rat Is Fond of Rice": "I love you like the rat is fond of rice..."

When he saw Yijun, he pointed to the seat beside him. "Here you are, Master Xiang. What do you like to drink?"

"Lemon tea." Yijun took off her overcoat and

sat down. "How come you invited me to the karaoke club?"

"No special reason. I just wanted you to sing with me."

"Why didn't you ask your girlfriend to keep you company?"

An smiled. "She's too busy."

Yijun cast a glance at him. "I see."

An handed over the song book to her. Yijun selected some songs without thinking. While she was singing, An listened attentively. Every time she finished a song, he clapped his hands in an exaggerated way. "Bravo! Master Xiang, you're an excellent singer."

Yijun sniffed and found An smelling like alcohol. "Did you drink?"

He shook his head and grinned. "Just a little. You can't call that drinking. I had only a taste of it."

Yijun stared at him for a while. She wanted to say something, but suddenly changed her mind.

"Shall I sing an aria of the Beijing opera for you?" An said abruptly.

Before Yijun could answer, he stood up, moved one foot backward, bent down a little, and displayed his orchid-shaped fingers in a nimble manner.

"What a riot of brilliant purple and tender crimson / Among the ruined wells and crumbling walls / What an enchanting sight on this fine morning / Whose is this courtyard where people can enjoy themselves—"

Yijun listened attentively. As he did not receive any professional training, he had a husky voice. He could not manage some of the high-pitched tones. Though he looked in her direction, he had a blank expression. It seemed to her that either he had gotten into the character that he was playing or he was singing without emotion. Yijun have had the opportunity of listening to all kinds of singing, professional and amateur, good and bad. However, it was the first time she had found somebody singing like this. She could not tell exactly how she was feeling. She was a bit saddened by his singing. She had no explanation for her mood.

After he finished the aria, An paused for a while before sitting down. He kept silent.

"I remember when I met you for the first time, you said my name sounded like that of a servant." he said a few minutes later.

Yijun corrected him. "It's not a servant. It's called

a domestic help."

An shook his hand. "Not much difference. You said Tang Bohu was renamed Hua An in order to court Qiu Xiang. Tang Bohu finally succeeded in marrying Qiu Xiang. He and I share the same given name 'An,' but he had much better luck than me."

"So, Master Xiang, what did you think of my singing?" An asked Yijun.

Yijun nodded her head. "Not bad."

An let out drunken belch. "I sang the same aria for her yesterday. Do you know what she said? She said, 'All your attempts to please me will prove futile. Even if you learn to sing all the arias of both the Beijing and Kunqu operas, we'll never be suitable for each other.' Master Xiang, if I had known this earlier, I would not have exerted my efforts to learn the traditional operas."

He managed a wry smile and bent his head to get the cigarette packet from his top pocket.

Yijun fixed her eyes on him, but kept silent.

He lit a cigarette. "It's said that traditional opera performers are usually a bit foolish. She is not foolish at all. I am the fool." He flashed her a weak smile. "Really, I'm a big fool."

He puffed at his cigarette and the smoke enveloped his face. As it was dim in the room, he looked a bit terrifying. Yijun found he was on the verge of tears and felt genuinely sorry for him. She hesitated for a moment before putting on a smile. She patted him on the shoulder. "Please spare me. Are you a fool? You're no fool at all. You've swindled many colleagues of mine into buying insurance policies, haven't you? How much have you earned in commission? I know you too well. You're very shrewd in business dealings."

She was about to go on when An lifted his head and stared at her. She felt a bit embarrassed and stopped speaking.

An smiled. "Master Xiang, you're really a good person."

Yijun was at a loss for what to say.

"Now I have to admit that traditional opera performers are usually a bit foolish," An started to say again.

Yijun pretended to be angry. "Hey, who are you calling foolish?"

An shook his head. "You're not foolish. You're lovely, Master Xiang. You're really lovely."

Yijun was touched. A flush rose to her cheeks. In order to hide her embarrassment, she turned sideways and took out a small mirror. She pretended to look at her face in the mirror. Unexpectedly, she saw in the mirror An staring at her with a smile. Her face was growing redder and it was impossible for her to hide it. She remained dazed for quite. "Don't call me 'Master Xiang' anymore. I feel shy with this form of address. From now on you just address me by name."

As soon as she completed the sentence, she felt her heart jump quickly as if it would leap out of her chest.

6

The airport Customs' annual buffet reception was held at the banquet hall of a five-star hotel in the downtown area. It would be the first time the new General Manager Tan would meet all his employees. As usual the leader gave a short address at the beginning of the reception. Mr. Tan was in his early forties. With a fair complexion and an amiable manner, he spoke in a soft, low voice.

While people were enjoying the delicious food, someone at the main table stood up and said in a loud voice, "Don't you know our general manager is good at singing the Beijing opera? How about inviting him to sing an aria for us?"

All those present gave him a round of applause. The general manager walked onto the platform and thanked the attendees in the Chinese way of greeting. He spoke into the microphone. "It's no fun singing alone. I suggest someone come up and sing together with me."

Someone said in a joking manner, "That's a good idea. A musical dialogue between two singers will be amusing. What about the aria 'A Couple Are on Their Way Back Home'?"

Someone else said, "Please spare me. That's an aria from the Huangmei opera. Our general manager is good at singing the Beijing opera. They are not of the same grade."

Yijun picked up a wrapper and put a piece of roast duck, scallion, and sweet sauce on it. Then she folded it up and was about to put it into her mouth when she heard the section chief say, "Xiang Yijun, what are you waiting for? Get onto the platform."

She was puzzled and slow to respond. Some of her colleagues were already calling out loudly, "We've got a Beijing opera singer here!"

Yijun was almost pulled up by her colleagues. After she stood up, she saw all the eyes in the room fastened on her. She tried her best to hide her slight embarrassment. When she got on the platform, she was so agitated that she did know where to put her hands.

"My young colleague, which aria shall we sing?" The general manager asked her.

"Why don't you decide," Yijun said.

"What about the aria 'Meditation in the Palace' from the Beijing opera *Yang Silang Visits His Mother*?"

Yijun nodded her head. "Since you ask me why I'm wearing a distressed expression / I do not dare to bare my heart to you / As two states are at war / My mother works for your enemy state / Now that she has escorted food and fodder to the front / I'd like to pay a visit to her / I don't know how to leave your state."

"You don't need to resort to sophistry / I won't stop you from visiting your mother."

"Even if you don't stop me / How can I pass the

borderline without an arrow token of authority?"

"I have intention to give you the arrow token of authority / But I'm afraid that you will never return."

"If you give me the arrow token of authority / I promise to return as soon as I see my mother."

"The camp of the Song state is far away from here / How can you return overnight?"

"Even if it's a long distance / I will ride at top speed and return in time."

"Just now you asked me to swear an oath / Now's time for you to take your oath."

Their theatrical dialogue drew loud applause. As this aria was sung at a quick tempo, it was very difficult for learners without a thorough basic training to have clear pronunciation. Yijun was surprised by the general manager's excellent performance. He was staring at her with admiration. They smiled at each other amiably.

Yijun went back to her seat.

"Since our new general manager is a fan of the Beijing opera, Yijun, fortune will be on your side," some colleagues said to her.

Yijun gave them a sardonic grin. "Do you really think fortune will smile on me just because our general manager likes to sing the Beijing opera?"

She sipped the orange juice in the glass. She found Ding Meimei looking at her without expression.

It was the Spring Festival. On the eve of the Chinese New Year, the deafening sound of firecrackers never ceased for the whole night. The room was permeated with the smell of gunpowder even when all the windows were tightly shut. After Xiang Hai got up on Lunar New Year's Day, he received a greeting call from the gum-chewing student. He wished Master Xiang all the best in the new year. He also asked Xiang Hai whether he could help him with changing the gas container or buying a bag of rice. Xiang Hai was moved and said he had gotten everything ready before the Spring Festival. He thanked him for his offer. After he hung up the phone, Xiang Hai wanted to go to the flower market. Seeing Yijun still sound asleep, he did not want to disturb her. He put on his coat and walked out of the room. Before he closed the door, he heard the stomping sound of footsteps. The young boy on the fifth floor rushed down the stairs. He paused in front of Xiang Hai and rushed downstairs without greeting him. A moment later, his mother hurried downstairs.

"You brat!" She shouted at the young boy. "Come back right now!"

The hallway was in an uproar.

Xiang Hai was shocked by the act of the son and his mother. It took him quite a while to find out what happened. He shook his head. He was about to go downstairs when the next door opened. Luo Manjuan walked out.

"Happy New Year!" She greeted him.

"Happy New Year," Xiang Hai returned her greeting immediately. "Are you going out?"

"Yes. I'm going to the market to get some vegetables."

Xiang Hai nodded his head. "I'm going to the flower market. Let's go together."

They walked slowly on the street. As it was not yet nine o'clock in the morning, there were not many people out. Though the temperature was low, it did not feel cold because of the warm sunshine.

"Are you going to visit your relatives during the Spring Festival?" Xiang Hai asked.

"My relatives live in other provinces," Luo Manjuan said. "Since my husband died, I've had little contact with his relatives. I'll spend the festival at home."

"I have nobody to visit except Yijun's uncle," Xiang Hai revealed.

Luo Manjuan sighed softly. "Only during the Spring Festival do I feel a little lonely,"

At first, Xiang Hai was at a loss for words when he heard her sad sigh. "A lonely life has its own benefits. Visits to your relatives and friends during the Spring Festival are disturbing and burdensome social etiquette."

"Do you think so?" Luo Manjuan asked. "On the contrary, I enjoy myself on these occasions."

Xiang Hai cracked a smile.

"I had better go in," Xiang Hai said when they reached the flower market.

"Goodbye," Luo Manjuan said.

They were about to part when Luo Manjuan suddenly stopped. "Master Xiang..."

Xiang Hai halted his steps immediately and looked at her. "Yes?"

Luo Manjuan smoothed out her hair. "If you and Yijun are free tonight, please come to my house and have dinner. Since we're neighbors and live close to each other, it will save you the trouble of cooking."

She spoke very quickly as if she was afraid she might not have the courage to finish. There was a faint flush on her cheeks and she felt ill at ease.

Xiang Hai felt awkward, too. "Well, I feel embarrassed because it will bring you a lot of trouble."

A part of him wanted to go and another part was reluctant. Luo Manjuan took his evasive remark as an affirmative answer. "It's no trouble at all. Several meat dishes are ready. I need only to cook two vegetable dishes."

Xiang Hai found it very difficult to decline her invitation. "OK, I'll bring a bottle of wine with me."

Luo Manjuan nodded her head.

Later that evening Xiang Hai and Yijun came to Luo Manjuan's home. Xiang Hai gave her with a bottle of dry red wine produced in 1994. Luo Manjuan was wearing an apron. Four plates of snacks—pistachios, preserved plums, preserved beef, and melon seeds— were set on the coffee table.

"Please sit and enjoy some appetizer," Luo Manjuan said. "Dinner will be ready soon."

Yijun offered to help her with the cooking but

Luo Manjuan pushed her out of the kitchen.

"There are not many dishes," she said. "I can manage by myself."

Her son Xiaowei was playing a video game in the corner of the room. He dutifully wished them a happy new year and then went back to concentrate on his video game.

The dining table was set. Cold dishes included salted sausages and pork, soy sauce braised beef, steamed gluten with black fungus, fried little yellow croakers, and shredded cucumber salad. A few minutes later Luo Manjuan served a plate of stir-fried green broccoli. Four of them sat at the table. Yijun poured some wine in each glass. Luo Manjuan said her son was too young to drink wine and poured a glass of coke for him. They clinked their glasses.

"I'd like to propose a toast to you for your hard work," Xiang Hai said to Luo Manjuan.

"It's nothing," Luo Manjuan said. "I'm only too glad to have you join us. You being here have made this New Year's Eve meal delightful. My son and I would have a lonely meal otherwise."

Then she turned to smile at Yijun. "Little girl, you'll be one year older tomorrow."

Yijun shook her head. "I'm getting old."

Luo Manjuan uttered a sound of surprise. "If you think you're old, what about me?"

"You grow more charming with maturity. We young girls are no match for you." Luo Manjuan smiled at Xiang Hai. "Master Xiang, you have a sweet and sensible daughter."

"She's by no means sensible," Xiang Hai said with a beam on his face. "She's a silly and unintelligent girl."

Then he took out a red packet from his pocket and put it in Xiaowei's hand.

Luo Manjuan hurriedly took the red packet from her son to return it to Xiang Hai. "That is not necessary."

"On the eve of New Year, it's a sign to express our hope for good luck," Xiang Hai said. "Please don't stand on ceremony with me."

Xiang Hai patted Xiaowei's head and gave him a smile. Luo Manjuan did not persist any further but gave Xiaowei an expectant look. "Say thank you to your uncle."

Xiaowei was eating a chicken wing. He raised his head and opened his mouth. "Thank you, Uncle!"

After dinner they chatted for a while. Then Xiang

Hai and his daughter said goodbye to Luo Manjuan.

"Master Xiang, what kind of flowers did you buy this morning?" Luo Manjuan asked all of a sudden.

"Lilies."

Luo Manjuan nodded approvingly. "The clear white lily looks graceful and gentle. I like it, too."

"I bought several multiple-bud lilies," Xiang Hai said. "Would you like to see them?"

"I'd love to. I'll come to your home as soon as I clean up the table."

Not long after Xiang Hai and his daughter got back home, Luo Manjuan came to their house. Fixing her eyes on the bunch of fragrant lilies on the side table, Luo Manjuan commented favorably and said the lilies were in perfect harmony with the elegantly furnished room. Xiang Hai asked her why she did not buy any flowers.

"Xiaowei is allergic to flowers and weeds," Luo Manjuan explained. "I can only grow asparagus fern and cactus."

Luo Manjuan offered to bring them some salted sausages and soy sauce braised beef. "I've salted too much meat. The salted meat will go moldy when it gets warmer. Master Xiang, please do me a favor by taking some of it."

"That's not necessary."

"We're neighbors," Luo Manjuan insisted. "You don't need to stand on ceremony. It will be a sin to waste food."

Xiang Hai had to accept her offer and said he would go to her home for it. Luo Manjuan nodded her head and went back home. After using the toilet, Xiang Hai went to Luo Manjuan's home. He found it funny that they both made two round trips in such a short time.

Luo Manjuan put some soy sauce braised beef and sausages in a plastic bag. "Master Xiang, you could have sent Yijun here for it. Why did you come by yourself?"

Xiang Hai thought she was right and that he should have let his daughter come for it. He stole a glance at Luo Manjuan and saw her just moving her eyes away from him. A faint smile spread over her face and it seemed that she was teasing him. After a brief hesitation, Xiang Hai took the plastic bag. "Thank you."

Luo Manjuan said nothing and opened the door for him. Xiang Hai went to the door and heard the greeting sound from the TV: "Wish you all the best! Wish you all the best!" He saw Luo Manjuan standing by his side. Clad in a light pink Tang-style costume, she was wearing a small golden hairpin. She was radiating all over. He was fascinated by her graceful manner.

"If they're to your taste, please come any time for more," Luo Manjuan said. "I have more than we can eat."

Xiang Hai thanked her again and went back home.

Before going to bed he went online. He told Liu Mengmei about his New Year's Eve meal at Luo Manjuan's home.

"Not bad," Liu Mengmei said. "It's almost like a family event."

"I did not have the heart to turn down her cordial invitation."

"Why don't you two form a new family?" Liu Mengmei asked. "That'll be good for the both of you."

Xiang Hai focused his eyes on the words on the screen but said nothing.

"Du Liniang, how old are you?" Liu Mengmei continued. "Are you fifty yet?"

"I'm 52."

"You're not too old. At your age I'm afraid you still need to satisfy that kind of desire, am I right?"

Xiang Hai meditated for quite a while before he understood what Liu Mengmei meant. A flush rose to his face. He looked around for fear that his daughter might come over. He found himself at a loss for words and thought his net pal had gone too far. Though net friends did not see each other during their net chat, they ought to let each other keep some self-respect. One should not talk in an unreserved manner.

After an initial hesitation, Xiang Hai changed the subject of conversation. "Did you have a happy New Year's Day?"

"Spring Festivals are the same every year," Liu Mengmei said. "You can't say one is happier than the other. I don't like the Spring Festival. Only children like to it."

Xiang Hai agreed. "That's true. The older you get, the less interest you'll have in the Spring Festival."

"Du Liniang, I bet that woman definitely likes to go to bed with you."

"How do you know?" Xiang Hai asked even

though he was shocked.

"If she has no desire to go to bed with you, how could she overflow with enthusiasm in inviting you to a dinner and giving you so much food? Du Liniang, it may be a good opportunity for you. Since the play goes as far as the episode "The Interruption of a Dream," you ought to make some substantial progress."

Emboldened by this audacious remark, Xiang Hai felt as though he could partly joke with Liu Mengmei. "Could you please teach me how I should act?"

"Do you really need a teacher? You're 52 years old. Why do you need me to teach you?"

"To tell the truth, I really don't know."

Liu Mengmei posted a big smiling face on the screen. "You ought to know what Du Liniang and Liu Mengmei do in their dreams. You and her can follow their example!" With these words he went offline.

Lately, Bai Wenli has felt something wrong with his throat. It seemed that there was phlegm blocking it. He could neither cough out phlegm nor swallow it. He bought some throat soothing medication at the pharmacy, but it did not work. Especially during the Spring Festival, many visitors came to wish him a Happy New Year and he was engaged in endless conversations every day. Gradually he felt his throat burning and he was running a temperature. He went to hospital and the doctor took an X-ray. Bai Weli found the doctor had a grave look when he examined the X-ray. He asked the doctor what was wrong with him.

"You've got a tumor in your throat," The doctor said.

A sinking feeling came over Bai Wenli. "Is it benign or malignant?"

"It's hard to tell now. The laboratory test result will come out next week."

Bai Wenli went back home. He did not reveal the truth to his wife for fear that she would be worried and make him even more worried. He was in low spirits. He spent the rest of the Spring Festival at home. He declined invitations to dinner. The dates were fixed for the taping of the last few episodes of the situation comedy. He had to be there. As he was in a restless mood, he had a slip of tongue very often. Sometimes, a scene had to be shot a dozen of times.

"Master Bai, did you drink too much during the Spring Festival that your tongue is not at your command?" Some well acquainted actors said to him jokingly.

He could not say anything but only gave a wry smile.

Bai Wenli received a greeting call from Yu Feifei. "Master Bai, Happy New Year!"

Yu Feifei did not hide her high spirits over the phone. "I wanted to take you out to dinner, but I've been so busy. You're my mentor. Without your advice and support, I would not be what I am today. I hope you will always enjoy good health and get what you long for."

After Bai Wenli hung up the phone, an idea occurred to him. He would like to visit Xiang Hai. He bought two bottles of brand name crab paste that was Xiang Hai's favorite food and a variety of fruits in a gift basket. He went to Xiang Hai's house.

"Why didn't you call me first?" Xiang Hai said, surprised. "What if I wasn't home?"

Bai Wenli smiled. "I know very well that you don't like social engagements and stay at home most of the time."

Xiang Hai laughed. "I'm not like you who have a lot of entertaining to do. You can always find me at my home."

Bai Wenli gave him a smile and sat down. "Is Yijun home?"

"She's at a get together with her old classmates," Xiang Hai said. "Young people are not like me, an old man who doesn't like to engage in too many social activities."

He turned on the TV and it was a special Spring Festival episode of the comedy entitled *Unconfirmed Stories about Old Uncle*. On the screen Bai Wenli, clad in a red Tang-style costume, was holding a basketful of fruits and was on his way to his friend's home for a New Year's Day courtesy visit. His over painted face was extremely shiny. A moment later he started to sing a few self-written lines to the tune of the Beijing opera: "Don't you see the Oriental Pearl TV Tower is shining with boundless brilliance / The Yangshan Harbor is long and tortuous / How can I not feel an upsurge of emotions / While at the finest hour..."

"Is there something wrong with your voice?" Xiang Hai asked as he listened attentively to Bai Wenli's singing.

"I have a touch of the flu."

Bai Wenli felt a sudden surge of warmth, thinking

that his senior co-learner was really an expert because nobody else could discover such a minor error in his voice.

"Being an actor, a good voice is fundamental. Since you have a touch of flu, you ought to take a rest at home," Xiang Hai said. "Why did you take the trouble to visit me?"

Bai Wenli was touched by Xiang Hai's sincere concern. "My senior co-learner, I had a dream last night. In my dream, we were practicing wushu together, exercising our voice together and catching sparrows together on the hill. Though our working conditions are much better now, I still cherish the memory of those heady days."

"You're saying this because you've experienced everything. I don't think you would have felt the same way twenty years ago."

Bai Wenli nodded his head. "You're right. Did you have a good Spring Festival?"

"Every Spring Festival is the same to me."

"Does Yijun have a boyfriend?"

"Not yet. She will be twenty-four years old the day after the Lunar New Year. Do you know any suitable young men?"

"Not for the time being. But I'll keep this in mind. I can assure you that I'll find an ideal boy for Yijun. He will be both comfortably off and morally qualified."

"Being comfortably off is of secondary importance. Being morally qualified is most important."

"Being comfortably off is not less important. As an old saying goes, the poor and lowly couple will be worn down by grief and misery. Being morally qualified alone can't ensure a happy life for Yijun."

Xiang Hai nodded his head. "I'll leave this matter to you."

The two co-learners had a pleasant conversation. Noon came before they knew it. All of a sudden, Bai Wenli's cell phone rang. He took out the phone to see his wife calling. She told him to come back home because two of his relatives living in another city are going to pay him a visit in the afternoon.

Bai Wenli stood up and said goodbye reluctantly. Xiang Hai opened the door for him. "Don't forget to see the doctor for the flu. You can't stand idle like this."

Bai Wenli uttered a sound of agreement and fixed his eyes on Xiang Hai. "My senior co-learner, come to my home when you're free. Let's have a heart-to-heart talk."

As soon as he uttered these words, a lump formed in his throat. He turned round and went down the stairs.

After closing the door, Xiang Hai recalled Bai Wenli's unusual expression. During the festive days he was in a melancholy mood. Xiang Hai sat down and watched TV for a few minutes. Then he turned his eyes to the closest tree outside the window, whose branches were faintly decorated with a couple of green leaves. As the Spring Festival fell on a date later than usual, the lunar seasonal division point "Beginning of Spring" had passed. Xiang Hai walked to the window. As soon as he opened the window, he was greeted by fresh air mixed with plant fragrance, moist soil, and mild warmth.

Another year had gone by. A year elapsed just like a page turned. Everybody's life was only a thin book and it would not take long to turn over its limited pages.

Somebody was knocking on the door. When Xiang Hai opened it he found Luo Manjuan standing in front of him. They kept silent while their eyes locked together. They stood still for quite a while before Xiang Hai showed her in. The faint smell of her perfume hung in the air. With a delicate smile, she fastened her expressive eyes on him. He immediately read her mind. For no apparent reason he kept fidgeting and his breath came in short gasps. He poured a cup of tea for her. She took the cup and their fingers touched each other. Both of them trembled a little. When their eyes met again, their facial expression changed completely.

Xiang Hai took out the purple brooch and pinned it on her sweater. His act was so intimate that he accidentally touched her breast. A blush came to his face first, and then a flush also rose to her cheeks. Both of them felt a sudden rush of emotion.

They went into Xiang Hai's bedroom. They went to bed together. It was difficult to tell who took the initiative. It was the natural outcome of their daily deepening relationship. They acted step by step just like a married couple of long standing. They did it in a calm and self-possessed manner as if they were very familiar with this routine.

Two sparrows were strolling on the windowsill in a leisurely manner. A gentle breeze came in and the rustled corner of the curtain looked like a billowing sail. The scene seemed to stir their emotions. All was quiet except the repeated greeting from the TV: "Wish you all the best! Wish you all the best—"

The Spring Festival was soon over.

Yijun was seriously perturbed when she recalled what had happened at the karaoke club the other night. She was waiting for An to lay bare their relationship. However, she had not heard from him for several weeks. He did not come to learn the Beijing opera, nor did he give her a call. Yijun intended to call him, but she gave up the idea because no girl ever took the initiative. She had to wait impatiently. She did not want to keep everything to herself, but she had to hold herself back. She knew there was something to look forward to, but she was not certain what.

Not until the Lantern Festival was over did she get a call from An. She was holding the cell phone with a throbbing heart.

"Did you have a nice Spring Festival?" An asked her

"It was so-so," Yijun said. "What about you?"

"I paid one visit after another to my clients. I

was fully occupied." Yijun said, "That's the way most people spend their Spring Festival."

While engaging in the conversation, Yijun was trying to figure out his intention. She just went along with the conversation.

"I have something to talk with you," An said after a moment of mindless chit chat.

Yijun's ears pricked up and her heart leapt with hope.

"I'm going to Chengdu," An said flatly.

Yijun was completely taken by a surprise. "Are you going there on business?"

"It's not a business trip. I've been transferred to the branch company there. Our manager promised to increase my salary by 30% and lease an apartment for me. I thought it was a good deal and accepted it."

Yijun was in a daze for quite a while.

"It's not a bad idea to go there," An continued. "I'll find a girlfriend among the Chengdu girls. They say that Chengdu girls have very beautiful skin and good temperaments. They're not like Shanghai girls. I think, if everything goes well, I may settle down there." He heaved a little sigh. "The only pity is nobody will teach me how to sing the traditional operas in Chengdu. Master Xiang, I loathe to part with you."

A lump formed in her throat when she heard this. She wanted to blurt out that he'd better stay in Shanghai then, but held herself back. She was no fool. She knew his real reason for moving to Chengdu. She was not Yu Feifei. How could she hold him back? It was awhile before Yijun could find her voice again and she managed to smile. "If you really loathe to part with me, I'll come to Chengdu to visit you when I'm on vacation. But you're responsible for the air ticket."

"No problem," An said. "When you come to Chengdu to teach me, let's sing the famous aria from *The Peony Pavilion*."

Yijun fought hard to hold her tears back. "OK."

Yijun was still left in a daze after she hung up the phone. But after some time she cracked a smile. She went to the bathroom and stared at her face in the mirror. She looked tired and weary. She stood still for awhile. All of a sudden, she pointed her orchid-shaped fingers at the girl in the mirror and said scornfully in the Beijing opera tone, "You, you're really stupid." The tears she fought back before started falling freely from her eyes.

7

With the approach of early summer and the Dragon Boat Festival, people started to shed the burden of their jackets. Plants grew lush and green. Birds flitted around and chirped joyously.

Ever since the Spring Festival Luo Manjuan had not offered Xiang Hai anymore wontons or chicken soup. She did not even say a word to him. Xiang Hai was well aware that she was waiting for him to make the first move, to say something first.

As the episode "The Interruption of a Dream" ends, which episode should be on next? Xiang Hai had no inkling what the next move should be. He had to bid for more time. He could not find anything appropriate to say or to do. His lengthy delay in making a decision strained their relations. When they met each other by accident in the hallway, they wanted to display a feeling of intimacy, but they were afraid they might go too far and arouse suspicions. As a result, they greeted each other with excessive politeness. They knew very well they were putting on a show. With the lapse of time they behaved even more overcautiously to each other than strangers.

In the blink of an eye, they broke up without any preliminary preparations.

Luo Manjuan returned the purple brooch to Xiang Hai. Xiang Hai intended to let her keep it, but did not know how to tell her. So he accepted it. It was raining that day. The constant rain was beating against the window.

"Master Xiang, my friend set me up on a date," Luo Manjuan said. "He works as an accountant at a securities company."

Xiang Hai was stunned but nodded his head. "That's good. The stock market is up. A securities company is sure to make a big profit. That's good."

Luo Manjuan shook her head. "I don't care whether he earns a lot of money. What counts most to me is that he is an honest family man. Master Xiang, I only want to marry a family man."

She found her voice becoming husky and she was on the verge of tears. She glanced at Xiang Hai's clean flawless cuffs. This man knew very well how to look after himself, why does he need a wife? She blamed herself for realizing this simple thing too late. The bunch of lilies on the side table looked graceful and exquisite and their sweet and delicate fragrance permeated the whole room. The sunshine came streaming in at the window and shone on the floor. This room seemed to be enveloped in mist, flooded with light and became dimly visible. Luo Manjuan thought of the salted pork and sausages hanging on the balcony. They had gone moldy due to humid weather. "Master Xiang, I've got to go." She ducked her head, turned round, and walked away.

Xiang Hai stared at her receding figure as he held the purple brooch in his hand. He had wanted to stop her from leaving. What could I do even if she stays? Xiang Hai knew very well they did not share the same feelings. He thought about how she mentioned "a family man" twice. He was embarrassed and disgusted, though he was not certain whether he was disgusted of her or of himself.

The gum-chewing student gave Xiang Hai a wicker basket of authentic Malu grapes grown by his uncle. Xiang Hai tried to politely decline to no avail, so he asked the student to stay for supper. The student provided Xiang Hai with an excuse to leave.

Before he said goodbye, the student mentioned the traditional opera school's performance plan for the next season. He asked Xiang Hai to put in a word for him and persuaded Principal Bai Wenli to cast him in a role. His request was beyond Xiang Hai's expectations. The student's frank and sincere remark embarrassed Xiang Hai instead. He promised to act on his behalf at the first opportunity. After the student left, Xiang Hai felt upset while looking at the wicker basket of grapes.

Not long after Yijun was transferred to the office of the general manager. As soon her new title became official, her colleagues teased her. "Yijun, now that you're promoted, please don't forget us in the future."

"It's not a promotion at all," Yijun said modestly. "It's just a simple transfer."

While she was sorting out her things, Ding Meimei, who sat opposite her, kept silent.

"Meimei, I hope you'll teach me how to dance when we're free," Yijun said to her.

The minute she uttered these words she regretted it. They did not suit the occasion.

Ding Meimei curled her lips. "What's the use of knowing how to dance? I was hoping you'd teach me how to sing traditional operas."

Yijun was embarrassed. She cracked a smile and said nothing. In March, the Customs organized a traditional opera singing contest for the sole purpose of pleasing the general manager. Yijun and the general manager sang an aria of *The Western Mansion* together, acting respectively the role of Zhang Sheng and Hong Niang. They won first prize. While accepting the prize, General Manager Tan was all smiles. "I do enjoy singing together with you. Unfortunately, you work in a different section. Otherwise we can sing together often."

"Why don't you transfer me to your office?" Yijun said with a smile.

Normally, she would never have the nerve to utter such a remark. She did not know why she had blurted that out. The general manager cast a stare at her and flashed her a smile.

Yijun sorted out her things and went out. Her colleagues' facial expression told her that she would replace Ding Meimei as the topic of their gossip. Yijun felt ill at ease, but in the meantime she had an indescribable feeling. She did not expect that her ability of singing traditional operas would produce such a wonderful effect. She was utterly confused because this was not what she had desired. She felt awkward, but also found it funny. Worldly matters were too complex to understand. They were not like the plot of a traditional play—either a love story between a talented scholar and a beautiful lady or a story about retribution for sin. Reality was much more complex and strange.

An emailed a photo of himself from Chengdu. He posed on a balcony, clad in a stage costume. Behind him rows of small houses were dimly visible. An told her he had bought this costume at a small shop and it cost him only a hundred yuan. He didn't expect that secondhand costumes would be sold in Chengdu. "Keep this as a souvenir." He wrote at the end of his email.

Yijun looked at this photo closely wondering who took the photo. Could it be possible that a Chengdu girl with beautiful skin took this photo? Yijun could not suppress a mirthless smile. All sorts of feelings welled up in her mind when she recalled the days she taught An how to sing the Beijing opera.

Bai Wenli was hospitalized after being diagnosed with throat cancer. Xiang Hai went to the hospital to pay him a visit. He had just undergone chemotherapy. He was so feeble that he could hardly speak. Xiang Hai told him to rest and promised to perform *Gathering of Heroes* with him after he recovered. As co-learners, they would perform just as good as when they first started to learn the traditional opera.

"I'm afraid I won't be able to live to see that day," Bai Wenli said with a forced smile.

Xiang Hai knitted his brows. "Your remark doesn't hold water. With the vigorous development of medicine, it's easy to transplant a liver or a heart, to say nothing of your minor disease. You must pull yourself together. If you yourself lose confidence, even a legendary doctor cannot save your life."

Xiang Hai put on an angry expression, but he felt sad at heart when he glanced at Bai Wenli's emaciated face.

"My senior co-learner, though I've been living a glorious life in recent years, I do like best the old days when we performed the Beijing opera together," Bai Wenli said as he looked out the window. "To tell you the truth, I cherished memories of those days."

Xiang Hai heaved a sigh and nodded his head. "As do I."

"My senior co-learner, has your wife Junyan been dead for twenty years?"

"It's been longer than that," Xiang Hai said. "It's already 23 years."

"When she died, she was almost the same age as Yijun now."

"You're right."

Bai Wenli became silent. Lying on the bed, he looked at the ceiling with a blank expression. A moment later he sang softly. "I look at myself in the mirror after I get up early in the morning / I do my hair with osmanthus-scented pomade / I paint my face by putting on peach-blossom powder / I apply apricot-pink rouge to my lips..."

His voice trailed off weakly as though he was talking in his sleeping.

Xiang Hai listened attentively and a girl's image appeared before his eyes. Clad in a flowery coat and black cloth pants, she was smiling so happily that her eyes looked like a crescent moon. When her face was bathed in the early morning sunshine, she seemed to be enveloped in golden light. Her smile was as brilliant as the sunshine. Lost in thought, Xiang Hai could not help follow Bai Wenli in humming: "I look at myself in the mirror after I get up early in the morning / I do my hair with osmanthus-scented pomade / I paint my face by putting on peach-blossom powder / I apply apricot-pink rouge to my lips..."

On his way back home from the hospital, Xiang Hai met the teenager living on the fifth floor who was fond of gambling. The teenager greeted him. After mumbling back a greeting, Xiang Hai was about to climb up the stairs when he heard the boy clear his throat. "Master Xiang, could you lend me some money?"

Xiang Hai was so surprised that he could not believe his ears. He turned his head to the boy. "What?"

The boy had a sly smile on his thin face. "Don't be so surprised. Let me put it in this way. Liu Mengmei wants to borrow some money from Du Liniang. Do you understand?"

Xiang Hai was nearly shocked speechless. "You..."

The boy cracked a cunning smile. "I'm asking for much money. Thirty thousand yuan will do. After you give me the money, I'll go back home immediately and delete all the chatting records. If you don't give me the money, I can't help you. As I will be killed sooner or later by the bookie, I'll have to upload your chatting records as a last resort. I'll also post your name and address so that you may enjoy great popularity in your old age." The boy uttered these words steadily with clear pronunciation. His well controlled rhythm sounded like that of Beijing opera articulation.

Xiang Hai felt as if all his blood had drained from his head. He was suddenly struck with a dizzy spell.

"So it's you. How can you...," Xiang Hai was unable to go on. His teeth were chattering and he was shivering all over. He stared at the boy with terror. He simply could not believe what was happening.

The boy flashed him another smile. "Thirty thousand yuan is not a lot of money to you. Your daughter works at the Customs and must be well paid. Master Xiang, I heard the woman downstairs is going to get married, is it true? As a matter of fact, I knew at the very beginning that you would not treat her seriously. You acted simply like you did on the stage. When the talented scholar and the beautiful woman get married, the play will be over. That's why your play is over. You and that woman are not of the same sort. In the old days, you might be a free-spirited and gifted scholar or a worldly Shanghainese whereas that woman might be only an ordinary housewife living in a lane house. I won't be free this afternoon. Tell me right now when you'll give me the money. I want cash only. I don't like transferring accounts." The boy looked at him, still smiling.

Xiang Hai was in a daze and did not know what to say. He felt dumb and stupid.

With the lapse of time, the end of the year was approaching.

Xilin called Yijun. She thought it was another invitation to play cards and answered before he could say anything. "I'm really busy."

"I'd like to take you to see that new Kunqu opera film *The Peony Pavilion*," Xilin said.

Yijun accepted his invitation after an initial hesitation.

The movie theatre had a full house. Seventy percent of the audience was young people. With aggressive promotion campaigns for TV, newspapers, and magazines, it became the most popular movie in Shanghai.

On the big screen, the young and beautiful Du

Liniang came to life in the garden.

"What a riot of brilliant purple and tender crimson / Among the ruined wells and crumbling walls / What an enchanting sight on this fine morning / Whose is this courtyard where people can enjoy themselves..."

Her father's singing of *The Peony Pavilion* echoed in her ears. For some unknown reason, it seemed to her that the two were not singing the same version of the play *The Peony Pavilion*. This Du Linang was entirely different from that Du Liniang. Yijun could not but laugh at herself for being so foolish. The play *The Peony Pavilion* was written by the ancient dramatist Tang Xianzu. How could one version be different from the other?

Yijun thought of An. She wondered if he would go and watch the film. She could not refrain from a grin when she recalled the way in he sang *The Peony Pavilion*. All of a sudden, Yijun realized that, in fact, everyone could sing *The Peony Pavilion*, such as Xiang Hai, Yu Feifei, Mao An, Bai Wenli, and herself. However, everyone's interpretation of *The Peony Pavilion* was different from others. A performer's own interpretation of "A Walk in the Garden" would produce his or her style of Du Liniang. Whether it was "the ruined wells and crumbling walls" or "an enchanting sight on this fine morning" depended on a performer's mind. Maybe this performer's enchanting sight on this fine morning was another one's ruined wells and crumbling walls.

"That was wonderful," Xilin said after the show was over. "The singing was very sweet."

Yijun noticed he had fallen asleep during the show. She did not bring this up and only cracked a smile instead.

"We should come again and see the other performances," Xilin said.

Yijun was thinking hard about how she should part ways with him.

"Can you teach me how to sing the Beijing opera?" Xilin asked abruptly when they reached the bus stop.

Yijun was taken by surprise.

"I know I'm not so refined and it may seem like I'm only fond of playing cards," Xilin said quickly. "I'm ignorant about art. But I'm modest, eager to learn, and smart. If you're willing to teach me, I'm sure I can learn how to sing the Beijing opera."

He appeared very nervous when he looked at Yijun. "Can you teach me?"

Yijun was at a loss. She had just been about to tell him that she would like to part company with him. She looked at his eyes. "Well...OK...since you have a husky voice, you should learn to act *laosheng* roles..."

She wondered what unknown force had driven her to say these words to him.

Yijun raised her head and saw the trailer for *The Peony Pavilion* shown on a huge screen at the top of the opposite high-rise. A beautiful young girl in an ancient costume was strolling with quick short steps in the garden decorated with beautifully ornamented pavilions and terraces. The frames of the film appeared dim and indistinct.

"What a riot of brilliant purple and tender crimson / Among the ruined wells and crumbling walls—"

All the pedestrians lifted their heads. The silky and plaintive singing reverberated in the sky as if a huge piece of thin gauze was enveloping the whole city. This piece of gauze rose on one side and fell on the other in the gentle breeze. It rippled softly and slowly, but spread far and wide.

Stories by Contemporary Writers from Shanghai

The Little Restaurant
Wang Anyi

A Pair of Jade Frogs
Ye Xin

Forty Roses
Sun Yong

Goodby, Xu Hu!
Zhao Changtian

Vicissitudes of Life
Wang Xiaoying

The Elephant
Chen Cun

Folk Song
Li Xiao

The Messenger's Letter
Sun Ganlu

Ah, Blue Bird
Lu Xing'er

His One and Only
Wang Xiaoyu

When a Baby Is Born
Cheng Naishan

Dissipation
Tang Ying

Paradise on Earth
Zhu Lin

The Most Beautiful Face in the World
Xue Shu

Beautiful Days
Teng Xiaolan